KU-265-074

BEFORE THE COFFEE GETS COLD
TALES FROM THE CAFE

Also by Toshikazu Kawaguchi

*Before the Coffee Gets Cold*

*Toshikazu Kawaguchi*

# BEFORE THE COFFEE GETS COLD
# TALES FROM THE CAFE

Translated from the Japanese by Geoffrey Trousselot

PICADOR

First published 2020 by Picador
an imprint of Pan Macmillan
The Smithson, 6 Briset Street, London ECIM 5NR
Associated companies throughout the world
www.panmacmillan.com

ISBN 978-1-5290-5086-8

Copyright © Toshikazu Kawaguchi 2017

Translation copyright © Picador 2020

The right of Toshikazu Kawaguchi to be identified as the
author of this work has been asserted by him in accordance
with the Copyright, Designs and Patents Act 1988.

Originally published in Japan as この嘘がばれないうちに
by Sunmark Publishing, Inc., Tokyo, Japan in 2017
Japanese/English translation rights arranged with Sunmark
Publishing, Inc., through Gudovitz & Company Literary
Agency, New York, USA

All rights reserved. No part of this publication may be reproduced,
stored in a retrieval system, or transmitted, in any form, or by any means
(electronic, mechanical, photocopying, recording or otherwise)
without the prior written permission of the publisher.

Pan Macmillan does not have any control over, or any responsibility for,
any author or third-party websites referred to in or on this book.

1 3 5 7 9 8 6 4 2

A CIP catalogue record for this book is available from the British Library.

Typeset in Giovanni by Jouve (UK), Milton Keynes
Printed and bound by CPI Group (UK) Ltd, Croydon, CRO 4YY

This book is sold subject to the condition that it shall not, by way of
trade or otherwise, be lent, hired out, or otherwise circulated without
the publisher's prior consent in any form of binding or cover other than
that in which it is published and without a similar condition including
this condition being imposed on the subsequent purchaser.

Visit www.picador.com to read more about all our books
and to buy them. You will also find features, author interviews and
news of any author events, and you can sign up for e-newsletters
so that you're always first to hear about our new releases.

*If you could go back, who would you want to meet?*

# Relationship map of characters

## Woman in the dress

A ghost who occupies the seat that returns you to the past. She leaves to use the toilet once a day. Usually she is found quietly reading her novel. But she curses anyone who disturbs her.

## Kiyoshi Manda

A detective working at Kanda Police Station. He bought his wife a birthday present but never gave it to her.

## Kimiko Manda

The wife of Kiyoshi Manda. She got caught up in a crime and just like that, she was killed.

## Kinuyo Mita

She was hospitalized with cancer six months ago. She never told Yukio about it – she didn't want to worry him. But her condition suddenly worsened, and she died.

## Nagare Tokita

Cousin of Kazu Tokita and owner of the cafe. He is a giant of a man, almost two metres tall.

## Kei Tokita

Wife of Nagare and mother of Miki. Six years ago, she died giving birth to Miki due to a weak heart.

## Miki Tokita

Daughter of Nagare Tokita and Kei Tokita. She is in first grade at elementary school.

## Yukio Mita

Son of Kunuyo Mita. He is studying under a famous ceramicist in Kyoto

*returned to the past*

## Kazu Tokita

Waitress of the cafe Funiculi Funicula. She serves the coffee during the ceremony that returns people to the past.

*returned to the past*

*returned to the past*

## Gohtaro Chiba

Runs a restaurant serving set Japanese meals. He raised Shuichi Kamiya's daughter after Shuichi died twenty-two years ago.

*came from the past*

## Katsuki Kurata

Three years ago, he fell ill. He was given only six months to live, and later died.

*colleagues*

## Fumiko Kiyokawa

A woman as beautiful as any celebrity. Seven years ago, she went back in time to meet the boyfriend who had left her at this cafe.

*returned to the past*

## Shuichi Kamiya

University friend of Gohtaro Chiba. He died twenty-two years ago, leaving his daughter an orphan.

## Asami Mori

Lover and work colleague of Katsuki Kurata. She is Fumiko's more junior colleague at work.

# CONTENTS

# I

## The Best Friend

Gohtaro Chiba had been lying to his daughter for twenty-two years.

The novelist Fyodor Dostoyevsky once wrote, 'The most difficult thing in life is to live and not lie.'

People lie for different reasons. Some lies are told in order to present yourself in a more interesting or more favourable light; others are told to deceive people. Lies can hurt, but they can also save your skin. Regardless of why they are told, however, lies most often lead to regret.

Gohtaro's predicament was of that kind. The lie he had told plagued him. Muttering things to himself, such as 'I never wanted to lie about it,' he was walking back and forth outside the cafe that offered its customers the chance to travel back in time.

The cafe was a few minutes' walk from Jimbocho Station in central Tokyo. Located on a narrow back street in an area of mostly office buildings, it displayed a small sign bearing its name, 'Funiculi Funicula'. The cafe was at basement level, so without this sign, people would walk by without noticing it.

Descending the stairs, Gohtaro arrived at a door decorated with engravings. Still muttering to himself, he shook his head, swung round and began walking back up the stairs. But then he suddenly stopped with a thoughtful expression on his face. He went back and forth for a while, climbing the stairs and descending them.

'Why not stew over it after you come in?' said a voice abruptly.

Turning around, startled, Gohtaro saw a petite woman standing there. Over her white shirt she was wearing a black waistcoat and a sommelier's apron. He could tell instantly she was the cafe's waitress.

'Ah yes, well . . .'

As Gohtaro began to struggle with his response, the woman slipped past him and briskly descended the stairs.

### CLANG-DONG

The ring of a cowbell hung in the air as she entered the cafe. She hadn't exactly twisted his arm, but Gohtaro descended once again. He felt a weird calmness sweep over him, as if the contents of his heart had been laid bare.

He had been stuck walking back and forth because he had no way of being certain that this cafe was actually *the* cafe 'where you could return to the past'. He'd come there believing the story, but if the rumour his old friend had told him was completely made up, he would soon be one very embarrassed customer.

If travelling back to the past was indeed real, he had heard there were some annoying conditions that you had to follow. One was that there was nothing you could do while in the past that would change the present, no matter how hard you tried.

When Gohtaro first heard that, he wondered, *If you can't change anything, why would anyone want to go back?*

Yet he was now standing at the front door of the cafe thinking, *Even so, I want to go back.*

Had the woman read his mind just now? Surely a more conventional thing to say in that situation would be, *Would you like to come in? Please feel welcome.*

But she had said, *Why not stew over it after you come in?*

Perhaps she meant: yes, you can return to the past, but why not come inside first before deciding whether to go or not.

The bigger mystery was how the woman could possibly know why he had come. Yet he felt a flicker of hope. The woman's offhand comment was the trigger for him to make up his mind. He reached out, turned the doorknob, and opened the door.

**CLANG-DONG**

He stepped into the cafe where, supposedly, you could travel back in time.

Gohtaro Chiba, aged fifty-one, was of stocky build, which was perhaps not unrelated to him having belonged to the rugby club in high school and at university. Even today, he wore an XXL-sized suit.

He lived with his daughter Haruka, who would be twenty-three this year. Struggling as a single parent, he had raised her alone. She had grown up being told, *Your mother died of an illness when you were little.* Gohtaro ran the Kamiya Diner, a modest eatery in the city of Hachioji in the Greater Tokyo Area. It served meals with rice, soup and side dishes, and Haruka lent a hand.

Entering the cafe through the two-metre-high wooden door, he still had to pass through a small corridor. Straight ahead was the door to the toilet, in the centre of the wall to the right was the entrance to the cafe. As he stepped into the cafe itself, he saw a woman sitting at one of the counter chairs. She instantly called out, 'Kazu . . . customer!'

Sitting beside her was a boy who looked about elementary school age. At the far table sat a woman in a white short-sleeved dress. With a pale complexion and a complete lack of interest in the world around her, she was quietly reading a book.

'The waitress just got back from shopping, so why don't you take a seat. She'll be out soon.'

Obviously caring little for formalities with strangers, she spoke to Gohtaro casually, as if he was a familiar face. She appeared to be a regular at the cafe. Rather than replying, he just gave a little nod of thanks. He felt the woman was look-ing at him with an expression that seemed to say, *You can ask me anything you like about this cafe.* But he chose to pretend he hadn't noticed and sat down at the table closest to the entrance. He looked around. There were very large antique wall clocks that stretched from floor to ceiling. A gently rotating fan hung from where two natural wooden beams intersected. The earthen plaster walls were a subdued tan colour, much like *kinako*, roasted soya flour, with a hazy patina of age – this place looked very old – spread across every surface. The windowless basement, lit only by shaded lamps hanging from the ceiling, was quite dim. The entire lighting was noticeably tainted with a sepia hue.

'Hello, welcome!'

The woman who had spoken to him on the stairs appeared from the back room and placed a glass of water in front of him.

Her name was Kazu Tokita. Her mid-length hair was tied back, and over her white shirt with black bow tie she wore a black waistcoat and a sommelier's apron. Kazu was Funiculi Funicula's waitress. Her face was pretty with thin almond eyes, but there was nothing striking about it that might leave an impression. If you were to close your eyes upon meeting her and try to remember what you saw, nothing would come to mind. She was one of those people who found it easy to blend in with the crowd. This year she would be twenty-nine.

'Ah . . . um . . . Is this the place . . . that er . . .'

Gohtaro was completely lost as to how to broach the subject of returning to the past. Kazu calmly looked at him fluster. She turned towards the kitchen and asked, 'When do you want to return to?'

The sound of coffee gurgling in the siphon came from the kitchen.

*That waitress must be a mind-reader . . .*

The faint aroma of coffee beginning to drift through the room sparked his memory of *that day*.

It was right in front of this cafe that Gohtaro met Shuichi Kamiya for the first time in seven years. The two had been teammates who played rugby together at university.

At the time Gohtaro was homeless and penniless, having been forced to surrender all his assets – he had been the co-signer on a loan obligation for a friend's company that had gone bankrupt. His clothes were dirty, and he reeked.

Nevertheless, instead of being disgusted by his appearance, Shuichi looked genuinely pleased to have met him again. He invited Gohtaro into the cafe, and after hearing what happened, proposed: 'Come and work at my diner.'

After graduation Shuichi had been scouted for his rugby talent by a company in a corporate league in Osaka, but he hadn't played even one year before an injury cut short his career. He then joined a company that ran a restaurant chain. Shuichi, the eternal optimist that he was, saw this setback as a chance, and by working two or three times as hard as everyone else he rose to become an area manager in charge of seven outlets. When he got married, he decided to strike out on his own. He started a small Japanese restaurant and worked there with his wife. Now he told Gohtaro that the restaurant was busy and that some extra help would be welcome.

'If you accepted my offer, it would be helping me out too.'

Run down by poverty and having lost all hope, Gohtaro broke down in tears of gratitude. He nodded. 'OK! I'll do it.'

The chair screeched as Shuichi stood up abruptly. Grinning cheerfully, he added, 'Oh, and wait till you see my daughter!'

Gohtaro still wasn't married and he was a little surprised to hear that Shuichi had a child.

'Daughter?' he responded with his eyes widening.

'Yeah! She's just been born. She is so – cute!'

Shuichi seemed pleased with Gohtaro's response. He took the bill and strolled over to the cash register. 'Excuse me, I'd like to pay.'

Standing at the register was a fellow about high-school age. He was very tall, close to two metres in height, and had distant, thin almond eyes.

'Comes to seven hundred and sixty yen.'

'Here, from this please.'

Gohtaro and Shuichi were rugby players and bigger than most, but they both looked up at the young fellow, then looked at each other, and laughed, probably because they were thinking the same thing, *This guy is built for rugby.*

'And here's your change.'

Shuichi took the change and headed for the exit.

Before he was homeless, Gohtaro was quite well-off, having inherited his father's company that made over one hundred million yen a year. Gohtaro was a sincere kind of guy, but money changes people. It put him in a good mood, and he started squandering it. There was a time in his life when he thought that if you had money, you could do anything. But his friend's company to which he had co-signed as guarantor folded, and after being hit with this huge debt obligation his own company went under too. As soon as his money was gone, everyone around him suddenly started treating him like an outcast. He had thought those close to him were his friends, but they deserted him, one even saying openly to his face, *What use are you without money?*

But Shuichi was different; he treated Gohtaro, who had lost everything, as important. People willing to help someone struggling, without expecting anything in return, are rare indeed. But Shuichi Kamiya was one such person. As he followed Shuichi out of the cafe, Gohtaro was adamant in his resolve: *I'll repay this favour!*

**CLANG-DONG**

'That was twenty-two years ago.'

Gohtaro Chiba reached for the glass in front of him. Wetting his parched throat, he sighed. He looked young for fifty-one, but a scattering of grey hairs had begun to show.

'And so, I started to work for Shuichi. I put my head down and tried to learn the job as fast as I could. But after a year, there was a traffic accident. Shuichi and his wife . . .'

It had happened more than twenty years ago, but the shock of it had never left him. His eyes reddened and he began choking on his words.

*Sluurrrp!*

The boy sitting at the counter began noisily sucking the final drops of his orange juice through his straw.

'And what happened then?' Kazu asked matter-of-factly, not pausing in her work. She never changed her tone no matter how serious the conversation. That was her stance – her way of keeping herself at a distance from people, perhaps.

'Shuichi's daughter survived, and I decided to bring her up.'

Gohtaro spoke with his eyes cast down as if muttering to himself. Then he stood up slowly.

'I beg of you. Please let me go back to that day twenty-two years ago.'

He bowed long and deep, bringing his hips to a near right angle and dropping his head lower.

This was the cafe Funiculi Funicula. The cafe that became the subject of an urban legend some ten years ago as being the one where you could go back in time. Urban legends are made up, but it was said that at this cafe, you could really return to the past.

All sorts of tales are told about it, even today, like the one about the woman who went back to see the boyfriend she had split up from, or the sister who returned to see her younger sister who had been killed in a car crash, and the wife who travelled to see her husband who had lost his memory.

In order to go back to the past, however, you had to obey some very frustrating rules.

The first rule: the only people who you can meet while in the past are those who have visited the cafe. If the person you want to meet has never visited the cafe, you can return to the past, but you cannot meet them. In other words, if visitors came from far and wide across Japan, it would turn out to be a wasted journey for practically all of them.

The second rule: there is nothing you can do while in the past that will change the present. Hearing this one is a real let-down for most people and normally they leave in disappointment. That is because most customers who want to return to the past are wishing to fix past deeds. Very few customers still want to travel back after they realize they can't change reality.

The third rule: there is only one seat that allows you to go back in time. But another customer is sitting on it. The only time you can sit there is when the customer goes to the toilet. That customer always goes once a day, but no one can predict when that will be.

The fourth rule: while in the past, you cannot move from your seat. If you do, you will be pulled back to the present by force. That means that while you are in the past, there is no way to leave the cafe.

The fifth rule: your stay in the past begins when the coffee is poured and must end before the coffee gets cold. Moreover, the coffee cannot be poured by just anybody; it must be poured by Kazu Tokita.

Regardless of these frustrating rules, there were customers who heard the legend and came to the cafe asking to go back in time.

Gohtaro was one such person.

'Let's say that you do travel back to the past, what are you planning to do?' asked the woman who had told him to take a seat when he had entered. Her name was Kyoko Kijima. She was a full-time wife and mother, and a regular. It was just coincidence that she was in the cafe then, but she stared at Gohtaro with intense curiosity – perhaps he was the first customer she had met who wanted to return to the past. 'Forgive me for asking, but how old are you?'

'I'm fifty-one.'

Gohtaro seemed to have taken the question as a criticism, as in, *Why are you, a man of your age, blathering on about going back in time?* He sat hunched over the table staring fixedly down at his clasped hands.

'. . . I'm sorry. But don't you think it would be a little freaky? Totally unprepared, Shuichi, or whatever his name is, suddenly finds himself face-to-face with a twenty-two-year-older version of you?'

Gohtaro didn't lift his head.

Kyoko continued, 'Don't you think that would be a bit weird?'

She looked over the counter to Kazu for agreement.

'Well, maybe,' Kazu answered, in a manner that suggested she did not fully agree.

'Hey, Mum, isn't your coffee going to get cold?' muttered the boy, who was starting to fidget now his glass of orange juice was empty. His name was Yohsuke Kijima. He was Kyoko's son, and beginning this spring, he would be in grade four. His hair was mid-length and arranged untidily, he had a sunburnt face and he was wearing a sports strip that read 'MEITOKU FC' with the number 9 printed on the back. He was a football nut.

He was talking about the takeaway coffee in the paper bag on the counter beside Kyoko.

'Oh, it doesn't matter. Grandma hates hot drinks anyway,' Kyoko said as she moved her face up to Yohsuke's ear and whispered, 'Just wait a little longer and we'll go, OK?'

She glanced over at Gohtaro, anticipating a response of some kind.

Gohtaro was sitting up again, looking recomposed.

'Yeah, I guess it would freak him out,' he admitted.

'Uh huh,' responded Kyoko, nodding knowingly. While listening to this exchange, Kazu handed Yohsuke a new orange juice, which he silently accepted, with a quick nod of thanks.

'If it is the honest truth that you can go back in time, then there is something I really want to tell Shuichi.'

Though Kyoko had asked him the question, Gohtaro had answered looking at Kazu. His words had no effect on her expression.

Looking as nonchalant as always, she came out from behind the counter and stood in front of him.

Every now and then, a customer like Gohtaro would come to the cafe after hearing the rumour that you could travel back in time, and the way Kazu responded to each of them never changed.

'Are you familiar with the rules?' she asked briefly – there were customers who rolled up at the cafe with no idea of them.

'More or less . . .' he replied hesitantly.

'More or less?' Kyoko shouted. Of everyone in the cafe right now, she alone was a little excited. Kazu glanced at Kyoko without comment and then looked back at Gohtaro and stared. *Answer the question.*

Gohtaro shrugged apologetically. 'You sit in a chair, some-one makes you a coffee, and you return to the past . . . that's all I've heard,' he replied awkwardly. His nervousness must have left him dry-mouthed as he reached for the glass in front of him.

'That's a bit simplistic . . . Who'd you hear that from?' Kyoko quizzed him.

'From Shuichi.'

'If you heard it from Shuichi . . . eh? You mean you heard about it twenty-two years ago?'

'Yes, when we first came to this cafe, I heard it from Shu-ichi. He must have known of the legend.'

'I see . . .'

'So, even if a much-older version of me were to suddenly appear, apart from giving Shuichi a fright, I think it would be OK,' he said, returning to Kyoko's question.

'What do you think, Kazu?'

Kyoko spoke as if the right to decide for returning to the past belonged to her and Kazu alone. But Kazu did not com-ment. Instead, she spoke in a cool, stern manner.

'You know that even if you return to the past, reality won't change, right?'

What she meant was, *You know you can't stop your friend from dying!*

So many customers had come to the cafe hoping to go back and prevent someone from dying. Each time, Kazu explained this rule.

It wasn't that she was impervious to the grief that people felt from losing someone precious to them. There was just no getting around this rule – no matter who you were, regardless of your reason.

Having heard Kazu's words, Gohtaro showed no sign of agitation.

'I am aware of that,' he replied in an even-tempered, soft voice.

### CLANG-DONG

The doorbell rang. A girl. When Kazu saw her, instead of saying, *Hello, welcome*, she said, 'Welcome home!'

The girl's name was Miki Tokita, daughter of the cafe's owner, Nagare Tokita. She was proudly bearing a bright red *randoseru* elementary-school backpack.

'*Moi* is back, darlings!' Miki announced in a voice that reverberated loudly throughout the cafe.

'Hello, Miki darling! Where did you get that wonderful *randoseru*?' Kyoko asked.

'She bought it for *moi*!' Miki said smiling broadly, pointing at Kazu.

'Wow! It looks fantastic!' complimented Kyoko.

Kyoko looked at Kazu. 'Doesn't school start tomorrow?' she asked in a quiet whisper.

She didn't mean to criticize Miki's conduct, nor did she mean to poke fun at her. In fact, it genuinely brought a smile to her face that Miki was so happy to have received a brand-new *randoseru* that she had been parading around the neighbourhood with it on her back.

'Yes, it's tomorrow,' Kazu said, also pursing the beginnings of a smile in the corners of her lips.

'How is Madame Kinuyo? Is she well?' Miki asked, still carrying on the conversation in a voice loud enough to reverberate through the cafe.

'Mrs Kinuyo is well! We've come into the cafe again today to pick her up another coffee and sandwich made by your daddy,' Kyoko said while holding up the paper bag holding the takeaway beside her. Sitting on the next stool along, Yohsuke kept his back to Miki, and slowly sipped his second glass of orange juice.

'Isn't Mrs Kinuyo tired of eating Daddy's sandwiches yet? That's all she's been eating every day.'

'Mrs Kinuyo says she loves your daddy's sandwiches and coffee.'

'I don't know why. Daddy's sandwiches are not that tasty,' remarked Miki, still in a loud voice.

Overhearing the conversation, a towering figure appeared from the kitchen.

'Hey, hey! Whose sandwiches did you say were yucky?' It was Nagare, the cafe's owner and Miki's father. Miki's mother Kei was no longer with them. She had a weak heart and passed away after giving birth to Miki six years ago.

'Oops-a-daisy, well, darlings, I think *moi* will go now,' said Miki in her camp way. She bowed her head to Kyoko and scampered off to the back room.

'Moi . . . ?'

Kyoko looked at Nagare as if to ask, *Where did she learn that?*

Nagare shrugged. 'Beats me.'

Giving a sideways glance at Kyoko and Nagare, Yohsuke started poking at Kyoko's upper arm.

'Can we go now?' he asked, sounding like he was fed up with waiting around.

'Oh, we were about to go, weren't we,' Kyoko said, acknowledging that they should get a move on, and got up from the counter stool.

'Well, it's time for *moi* to go too, darlings,' Kyoko said, mimicking Miki.

She gave the paper bag to Yohsuke and without looking at a bill, she placed the money for the sandwich and coffee and for Yohsuke's drink on the counter, including the second orange juice that Kazu poured him.

'The second orange juice is on the house,' said Kazu as she took the money from the counter minus the price of the second orange juice and started to press the cash register keys loudly.

'No, no. I'll pay.'

'You don't pay for what you don't order. I just gave it to him.'

Kyoko didn't want to pick up the money remaining on the counter, but Kazu had already put the rest in the till and handed Kyoko a receipt.

'Oh . . . OK.'

Kyoko wasn't comfortable not paying for the drink, but she knew there was no way Kazu was going to accept payment.

'Well, if you say so,' she said as she picked up the money for one orange juice from the counter. 'Thank you.' She returned the money to her purse.

'Send my regards to Kinuyo sensei,' said Kazu, politely bowing to Kyoko.

Kinuyo had taught Kazu painting since she was seven. It was Kinuyo who had encouraged her to study to get into a fine arts university. After graduating, Kazu had begun working part-time at Kinuyo's painting school. Now Kinuyo was hospitalized, Kazu was teaching all the classes.

'I know you're busy here too, so thank you so much for taking the art classes again this week.'

'Of course, not a problem,' Kazu replied.

'Thank you for the orange juice,' Yohsuke said nodding towards Kazu and Nagare, who were both standing behind the counter. Yohsuke left the cafe first.

CLANG-DONG

'OK, I'll be off.'

Kyoko waved goodbye and followed Yohsuke out of the door.

CLANG-DONG

When the two left the cafe, so did the lively atmosphere, leaving the room silent. The cafe did not play background music, which meant when no one was talking, you could hear the woman in the white dress turning the pages of her novel.

'How did they say Kinuyo was getting along?' Nagare asked Kazu as he stood polishing a glass – his tone no different than if he had been talking to himself. Kazu slowly nodded her head once but she didn't answer his question.

'I see,' Nagare said softly and then disappeared off into the back room.

Left in the cafe were Gohtaro, Kazu and the woman in the white dress.

Kazu was behind the counter tidying up in her usual way.

'I'd like to hear more now, if it's all right with you?'

Kazu was ready to listen to Gohtaro's reason for returning to the past.

He looked up at her for an instant then immediately averted his eyes. He took a slow deep breath.

'. . . Actually,' he began, suggesting that perhaps earlier he had been purposely holding back about his reasons. Maybe because Kyoko was just a bystander, and it was none of her business.

But now, apart from the woman in the white dress, it was just Gohtaro and Kazu. He began explaining hesitantly.

'My daughter is getting married.'

'Married?'

'Yeah, I mean . . . really, she's Shuichi's daughter,' he mumbled. 'I want to show my daughter who her real father was.' He brought out a very slim digital camera from his suit pocket. 'I thought if I could record a message from Shuichi . . .' He sounded lonely and small.

Kazu stared at him in this state. 'What happens afterwards?' she asked quietly. She wanted to know what would happen after he revealed that he was not her true father.

Gohtaro felt a jolt in his heart.

*This waitress won't be fooled by lies.*

He spoke while staring into space, as if he had prepared his answer. 'I can only see it being the end of my role,' he said with quiet resignation.

Gohtaro and Shuichi were in the same rugby team at university, but they had known each other since they began rugby training back in elementary school. They played in different teams, but occasionally they would meet at a match. That isn't to say they noticed one another right from the start. Through junior high and high school, they were playing for their respective schools, competing in opposing teams in official matches, and so gradually became aware of each other's existence as a result.

By chance, they entered the same university and became teammates. Gohtaro was a fullback while Shuichi was a fly-half.

The fly-half, identified by the number 10 on his back, is the star player in rugby. He is like the fourth player in the batting order or a pitcher in baseball, or the striker in football. Shuichi was amazing as a fly-half, and he earned the nickname Shuichi the Seer because his plays during matches were like miracles – players even remarked that it was as if he could see into the future.

A rugby team has fifteen players, and there are ten positions. Shuichi took note of the other players' strengths and shortcomings, and he had a talent for knowing how to utilize or exploit any player in any position. This earned him the absolute trust of the senior players of the university rugby club, and they began to see him as a candidate for team captain early on.

Gohtaro, on the other hand, had tried various positions

since he first began playing rugby in elementary school. He was not the type of person who could easily say no to people's requests, and would often fill in when the team was short of a player. The person who finally decided that full-back was the best position for the versatile Gohtaro was Shu-ichi. The fullback was the last bastion of defence, and thus very important. If any of the opposition breached his team's line of defence, his job was stop them with an effective tackle and prevent them scoring a try. Shuichi wanted Gohtaro for fullback because of his superior tackling ability. When he played against Gohtaro in official matches in junior high and high school, he was never once able to slip past him. If the team had Gohtaro's formidable tackling, there would be absolutely nothing to worry about. It was his steel-wall defence that enabled Shuichi's daring offensive plays.

*When I leave the back to you, I know I've got someone I can count on*, Shuichi often said before a match.

Then, seven years after they graduated from university, the two met again by chance.

After leaving the cafe, they headed off to Shuichi's apartment. There to greet them were Yoko and their newborn daughter, Haruka. Shuichi must have contacted Yoko on the way, as she had run a bath for Gohtaro.

Yoko greeted him – still unwashed and reeking – with a warm smile. 'So you are Gohtaro the Fullback? Shuichi has spoken of you countless times.'

Osaka-born Yoko was even more accommodating than Shuichi. It was quite normal for her to spend every waking hour chatting, and she enjoyed making people laugh with her jokes. She was also quick-thinking and proactive. In less than a day she had found Gohtaro a place to live and clothes to wear.

After losing his company, Gohtaro had lost his ability to trust people, but just two months after starting at Shuichi's restaurant, he was back to his bright and cheerful self.

When the restaurant was filled with regular customers, Yoko would talk Gohtaro up: 'Back at university, he was my husband's most trusted player.'

While he found that embarrassing, it also brought a smile to his face. 'My next task is to earn the same reputation working here,' he once added, his newly brightened outlook on the future on display.

Everything seemed to be going well.

One afternoon, Yoko complained of a screaming headache, so it was decided that Shuichi would drive her to the hospital. They didn't want to close the restaurant, so Gohtaro stayed while minding Haruka. That day, petals from the cherry blossoms were scattering across the cloudless blue sky, silently, like a flurry of snow.

'Look after Haruka for me,' Shuichi said, waving thanks while hurrying out.

That was the last time Gohtaro saw him.

Shuichi's and Yoko's parents and grandparents were all dead, so at the age of one, Haruka was left all alone in this world.

When he looked at Haruka's smiling face at Shuichi's funeral – too young to comprehend that both her parents had died – he decided there and then to raise her himself.

*Dong, dong, dong* . . .

A wall clock chimed eight times.

Startled by the sound, Gohtaro looked up. His eyelids were heavy, and his vision was blurry.

'Where . . . ?'

Looking around, he could see the cafe interior infused with a sepia hue by the shaded lamps. A fan hanging from the ceiling rotated slowly. The pillars and beams were coloured a deep brown. There were three large, and clearly very old, wall clocks.

It took him a while to come to the conclusion that he had been asleep. He was alone in the cafe, apart from the woman in the dress.

He patted both cheeks with his hands to untangle his memory. He remembered that Kazu had told him, 'We don't know when the chair that you use to return to the past will be empty.' Then he must have drifted off to sleep.

It seemed odd to him that he would doze off like that, having just made a decision as momentous as returning to the past. But he also couldn't help having doubts about the waitress who had left him alone in that state.

Gohtaro stood up and called out to the back room.

'Hello . . . is anyone there?'

But there was no reply.

He looked at one of the clocks on the wall to check the time, but then immediately checked his watch. The antique clocks in the cafe were the first strange thing one noticed when visiting. Each one showed a different time.

Apparently, the clocks at either end of the room were broken. One of them was fast, and the other, slow. Multiple attempts had been made to fix them, to no avail.

'8:12 p.m. . . .'

Gohtaro looked over at where the woman in the white dress was sitting.

Among the tales of this cafe that he had heard from Shuichi, there was one that had stuck in his mind: *A ghost is sitting in the chair that returns you to the past.*

The notion was quite preposterous and impossible to believe. That was why it had stuck in his mind.

Oblivious to Gohtaro's gaze, the woman read her novel with unfaltering concentration.

As he looked at her face, he began to feel a strange sense of recognition, as if he had met her somewhere before.

However, he couldn't see how that was possible if she truly was a ghost, so he simply shrugged it off.

*Flap.*

Suddenly, the woman in the dress closed the novel, the sound reverberating throughout the silent cafe. At her unexpected move, Gohtaro's heart nearly leaped out of his mouth, and he almost slipped off his seat at the counter. If she was just a normal human customer, her movement would probably not have shaken him so, but having been told that she was a ghost . . . He didn't believe she was, of course, but the image of 'ghost = creepy' couldn't be easily shaken once it had taken hold.

Momentarily petrified, he felt a cold clamminess spread up his spine. Ignoring Gohtaro's reaction, the woman rose without a sound. She slipped out of her seat and walked silently towards the entrance, clasping the novel she had been reading as if it was precious to her.

Feeling his heart pounding, Gohtaro watched her pass.

She went through the entrance and disappeared to the right. The only thing in that direction was the toilet.

*A ghost who goes to the toilet?*

Gohtaro tilted his head as he looked at the woman's chair. The seat that would take him back in time was vacant.

Tentatively taking one step at a time, he went over, constantly wary that the woman in the dress might suddenly reappear with a diabolical grimace.

Inspecting it up close, he saw it was a simple seat with nothing out of the ordinary about it. The chair had elegantly curved cabriole legs, and its seat and back were upholstered with a pale moss-green fabric. He was certainly no expert in antiques, but he could tell it would be worth a lot of money.

*If I were to sit on that chair . . .*

As soon as he placed his hand timidly on it, he heard the sound of scuffling slippers coming from the back room.

He turned and saw a girl wearing pyjamas. If he remembered correctly, she was the cafe owner's daughter, Miki. She stared at him with her big round eyes – she didn't seem at all shy about making eye contact with adults she didn't know. Confronted with her straight stare, Gohtaro was the one who felt uncomfortable with the eye contact.

'Good . . . good evening,' he said in a forced, unnatural voice, as he pulled his hand back from the chair. Miki scuffled towards him.

'Good evening, monsieur, do you want to return to the past?' she asked, peering at him with her big eyes.

'Ah, well, you see . . .'

Gohtaro was floundering, not sure how to answer that question.

'Why?'

Miki tilted her head inquisitively, ignoring how flustered he seemed.

He was anxious that the woman in the dress would return while he was talking to Miki.

'Could you call a member of staff?' he asked her.

Miki, however, completely ignored his request and instead slipped past him and stood in front of the seat in which the woman in the dress had been sitting.

'Kaname has gone to the toilet,' she said, shifting her gaze from the empty seat to Gohtaro.

'Kaname?'

Miki silently looked at the cafe entrance. Gohtaro followed her gaze and understanding, nodded. 'And her name's Kaname?'

But instead of answering, Miki pulled on his hand. 'Sit down,' she urged.

In a businesslike fashion, she cleared the woman's coffee cup and scuffled off in her slippers, disappearing into the kitchen and giving him no chance to protest.

He stared after her in blank amazement.

*Is she going to help me go back to the past?* he wondered. With an anxious expression, he slipped between the chair and the table in front of him and sat down.

He didn't know what he had to do to go back, but he felt his heart race at the thought that he was sitting in the chair.

After a while, Miki returned carrying a silver kettle and

white coffee cup, clattering on a tray she held with both hands.

She stood next to Gohtaro.

'Now *moi* will pour you the coffee,' she said as the tray wobbled.

*Can you really do this?* Gohtaro almost asked, but he held it in.

'Um . . . er,' he replied with a very anxious expression.

Miki didn't see the look on his face as she had fixed her big excited eyes on the cup on the tray. She continued with her explanation.

'In order to go back to the past . . .'

At that moment, Nagare, wearing a T-shirt, appeared from the back room.

'Heavens above, Miki, what do you think you're doing?' he said with an exasperated sigh. More than angry, his tone conveyed something more along the lines of, *Oh no, not again.*

'*Moi* is serving monsieur his coffee.'

'There is no way you can do that yet. And stop calling yourself *moi*.'

'*Moi* shall serve it.'

'Stop it. Now!'

While still holding the wobbling and rattling tray precariously, little Miki blew her cheeks out and looked up at giant Nagare.

Nagare's thin almond eyes narrowed and the corners of his mouth dropped into a frown as he looked down at Miki.

It felt like a standoff between the two, as if whoever spoke next would lose.

Kazu, who had appeared without anyone noticing, walked out from behind Nagare and knelt down in front of Miki.

'*Moi* . . .'

As Kazu looked her straight in her eyes at her level, Miki's big eyes gradually transformed from angry to teary. In that moment Miki seemed to realize she had lost.

Kazu smiled warmly at her.

'Your time will come,' she said as she quietly took the tray.

Miki looked up at Nagare, teary eyed. 'Uh-huh,' he simply said, and gently held out his hand. His face looked far less stern now.

'As you wish,' said Miki as she took hold of the hand stretched out to her and drew to his side. The defiant expression she had worn until just moments ago had dissipated. When Miki got annoyed and upset like this, she could quickly switch her mood, rather than letting it drag on. Observing her transformation, Nagare thought how like her mother she was, with a melancholic smile.

Based on how Kazu treated Miki, Gohtaro deduced, *This waitress is not the girl's mother.* He could also sympathize with how Nagare was struggling to handle a girl of this age – having had, after all, his own experience of raising his daughter Haruka as a single father.

'Let's go through the rules,' Kazu said softly next to Gohtaro, who was still sitting in the right seat.

The cafe was silent as always. Gohtaro had heard the rules from Shuichi some twenty-two years ago, but he could barely remember them now.

What he did remember was: that you go back in time, that reality won't change, no matter what you do, and that there was a ghost sitting on the chair. He was unclear on any other details. That Kazu was going to explain them to him was therefore welcome news.

'The first rule is that even though you can return to the past, you can only meet people who have visited this cafe.'

This rule didn't surprise him. It had been Shuichi who had invited him to the cafe. There was no doubt that he had been there.

As Gohtaro's face showed no sign of worry, Kazu briskly continued. She told him that when he went back he would not be able to change reality, no matter how hard he tried; that the only way to return to the past was by sitting where he sat; that he could not get up from the seat because if he did, he would be forcibly brought back to the present.

The bit about leaving the seat had been met with an 'Oh really?' from Gohtaro. But the rules were mostly as he had expected, and nothing drained the colour from his face.

'OK, I understand,' he said.

'Please wait while I remake the coffee,' Kazu instructed him when she had finished her explanation, and went into the kitchen.

She left him sitting there, with Nagare standing in front of him.

'Excuse my nosiness, but she is not your wife, is she?' he asked Nagare.

It wasn't as if he really needed to know the answer; it was more an attempt to make conversation.

'Her? No, she's my cousin,' Nagare replied, looking down at Miki.

'Miki's mum . . . Well, when she gave birth to her . . .'

Nagare didn't continue – not because he was choked with emotion, but simply because he thought he had already conveyed the message.

'I see . . .' said Gohtaro, and stopped asking questions. He looked at Nagare with his thin eyes, and then at Miki with her round eyes, and concluded that she must take after her mother. Caught up in that thought, he waited for Kazu.

Kazu soon returned. On the tray she was carrying were the same silver kettle and white coffee cup she had taken back into the kitchen. The aroma of the coffee, freshly made, drifted throughout the cafe and seemed to penetrate Gohtaro's chest deeply.

Kazu stood beside the table where Gohtaro was seated and continued the explanation.

'I will now serve you the coffee,' she said as she placed the white cup in front of him.

'OK.'

Gohtaro looked down at the blemish-free cup and was transfixed by its pure almost translucent whiteness. Kazu continued.

'The time you have in the past will only be from when I pour you the coffee until the coffee has gone cold.'

'OK.'

Perhaps because Gohtaro had been told the rules by Shuichi, the news that he could only return to the past for such a short period did not seem to surprise him.

Kazu gave a small nod.

'That means that you must drink the coffee before it gets cold. If you don't drink it then . . .' she continued.

She now had to explain, *You will become a ghost and go on sitting in this seat.* It was this rule that made returning to the past extremely risky. Compared to the great risk of becoming a ghost, not being able to meet who you wanted to meet, or not being able to change reality, were trifling inconveniences.

Yet, if Kazu was careless with her explanation, her words could be misconstrued as just a joke. To ensure she gave these words the gravitas they needed, she paused before she went on.

'You turn into a spook, right?' Gohtaro interrupted with those insane-sounding words.

'Huh?' asked Nagare, who was listening from a distance.

'A spook,' repeated Gohtaro without hesitation.

'When Shuichi told me the rules, that one was so crazy . . . er, excuse me . . . it was so difficult to believe, I remembered it clearly.'

From past experience, when a customer had not followed this rule, the damage was severe, and rather than thinking of the customer who became a ghost, Nagare was thinking about the people who get left behind. If it happened to Gohtaro, it would be a devastating shock to his daughter Haruka.

Yet for some reason, Gohtaro did not seem to acknowledge the seriousness of it, and throwing around words like *spook* suggested he wasn't taking it seriously. But Gohtaro's eyes looked serious, so rather than simply telling him that was wrong, Nagare's answer was vaguer.

'Er . . . nah . . .' he struggled to reply.

But Kazu's answer was plain.

'That's right,' she confirmed coolly.

'Eh?' uttered Nagare in surprise at her answer. His almond-shaped eyes opened wide, and his mouth dropped open. Miki standing next to him, who probably didn't know what a spook was, looked up at Nagare, her round eyes goggling.

Kazu, however – unbothered by Nagare's agitation – continued to explain the rules.

'You must not forget. If you do not finish drinking the coffee before it goes cold, it will be your turn to be the spook for ever stuck sitting here.'

It was true to Kazu's relaxed and generous nature to use Gohtaro's word spook, but she probably just went with the term because it was easier to do so. At any rate, it was clear what she meant: whether you called it a spook or a ghost, it was the same thing.

'So, the woman who has been sitting on the chair up until now?' Gohtaro asked, hinting, *She didn't return from the past, then?*

'. . . Yes,' Kazu confirmed.

'I wonder why she didn't finish her coffee?' Gohtaro asked. He asked purely out of interest. But his question turned Kazu's face into a Noh mask, and for the first time he found her expression unreadable.

*I've asked something I was not meant to ask*, Gohtaro thought, but Kazu wore this expression only for a moment and continued.

'She went back to meet her husband who had died, but she must have lost track of time and only realized when the coffee had already gone cold,' she stated with an expression that implied that there was no need for her to say what happened next.

'Oh, I see,' Gohtaro replied with a rather sympathetic expression. He looked over to the entrance through which the woman in the dress had disappeared.

He asked no more questions, so Kazu asked, 'Shall I serve?'

'Yes please,' he answered with a sigh.

Kazu took the silver kettle that was still on the tray. Gohtaro knew nothing about tableware, but he could see at a glance that this sparkling silver kettle would be worth a substantial sum. Kazu announced, 'Then I shall begin.'

As she uttered these words, Gohtaro felt that her aura had changed.

The temperature in the cafe seemed to suddenly drop by a degree and you could cut the atmosphere with a knife.

Kazu lifted the silver kettle up a little higher and uttered the words, 'Drink the coffee before it goes cold,' and then slowly began lowering the spout towards the cup. She moved with an impenetrable beauty, as if she was performing a solemn ritual.

When the spout was just a few centimetres from the cup, a threadlike column of black coffee appeared. It was soundless, and it didn't appear to be moving; only the surface of the liquid in the cup rose. The coffee that filled the vessel resembled a pitch-black shadow.

Transfixed by this beautiful sequence of movements, Gohtaro saw a plume of steam rise from the cup.

As he watched the steam, a strange sensation, much like dizziness, enveloped him, and everything surrounding the table began to ripple and shimmer.

Worried that another wave of sleepiness was coming on, he tried to rub his eyes.

'Argh . . .' he exclaimed unintentionally.

His hands, his body, were becoming one with the steam from the coffee. It had not been his surroundings that were rippling and shimmering; it had been him. Suddenly, his surroundings began to move so that everything above him was falling past him with amazing speed.

Experiencing all this, he screamed out, 'Stop . . . stop!'

He was no good with scary rides – the mere sight of them was enough to make him swoon – but unfortunately for him, his surroundings seemed to be going past him faster and faster, as time wound back twenty-two years.

He felt increasingly giddy. When he realized that he was now returning to the past, his consciousness gradually receded.

After Shuichi and his wife died, Gohtaro ran the restaurant alone while bringing up Haruka. Even while Shuichi was still alive, multitalented and diligent Gohtaro had worked out how to manage the restaurant single-handedly, from the cooking to the accounting.

But Gohtaro, a bachelor, found that raising a small child was unimaginably difficult. Haruka had just turned one – which meant she was now taking her first tentative steps – and someone needed to be watching her all the time. She would also often cry at night, which deprived him of sleep. When she entered nursery, he thought that life would become easier, but she became anxious around strangers and hated going. Every day she would burst into tears when it was time to leave.

When she was in elementary school, she would often announce she was going to help in the restaurant but only ended up being a nuisance. It was difficult to know by the words she used exactly what she meant, and if he didn't always listen to what she had to say she would sulk. If she got a fever, he had to take her to the doctor. And of course, children have a social calendar too, including birthdays, Christmas, Valentine's Day and so on. On holiday, it bothered him when she asked to be taken to a funfair, or say she wanted this and that.

In junior high, she entered her rebellious phase, which only grew worse with age. Once in high school, he received a phone call from the police after she had been caught shoplifting.

Adolescent Haruka got herself into all kinds of mischief, but however tense the circumstances, Gohtaro never once wavered in his resolve to provide a happy upbringing for her, who had been left alone in this world.

It was just three months earlier that she had brought home a man called Satoshi Obi and announced they were dating with the possibility that it might lead to marriage.

On his third visit, Satoshi asked Gohtaro, 'Please give me your blessing to marry Haruka.'

'You have my blessing,' he replied simply.

All he wanted was for her to be happy; he would not stand in the way of that.

After graduating from high school, Haruka became much more reasonable. She decided to go to culinary school to become a chef and that is where she met Obi. After finishing culinary school, Obi found a job in a hotel in Tokyo's Ikebukuro district and Haruka started helping at Gohtaro's restaurant.

After Haruka's wedding was announced, Gohtaro started to feel terrible guilt for lying to her.

For twenty-two years he had raised her, telling her that she was his real daughter. In order to hide from her the truth that she had no living blood relatives, he had never shown her the contents of the family register. But now she was to marry, everything was different. When she went to the registry office to file her marriage, she would discover that she was orphaned, revealing the lie that Gohtaro had maintained all these years.

After agonizing over it, he finally decided to tell her the truth before the wedding. Then he would say that the real father is meant to be there at the wedding ceremony.

*The truth will probably hurt her, but it can't be helped.*

Although there was nothing that could be done now.

'Ah, excuse me . . . Sir?'

Gohtaro awoke feeling his shoulder being shaken. A large-framed man stood in front of him. He was wearing jet-black school trousers and a dark brown apron over a white shirt with the sleeves folded to his elbows. Gohtaro recognized the giant as the cafe's owner Nagare. But it was a much younger Nagare.

The memory of that day started emerging from the re-
cesses of Gohtaro's brain.

He was certain that this young version of the owner,
Nagare, had been there twenty-two years ago.

The rest of the cafe, however – the slowly spinning ceiling
fan, the dark brown columns and beams and tan-coloured
walls and the three clocks on the wall each showing a different time – was unchanged. Even twenty-two years in the past,
the cafe had its sepia hue, the result of the only light being
given by the shaded lamps. If the young Nagare had not been
standing before him, he would not have noticed that he had
gone back.

However, the more he looked around the cafe, the faster
his heart beat.

*He's not here.*

If he had gone back to the right day, Shuichi should have
been there, but he wasn't.

He thought back to the various rules he had been told and
realized he had never been told how to return to the right
day. What's more, his time in the past was only the short
period before his coffee went cold. He might have arrived
before they arrived, or they may have already left the cafe.

'Shuichi!' Gohtaro called and without thinking began to
stand up. But before he did, he felt Nagare's big hand on his
shoulder keep him in his chair.

'He's in the toilet,' he muttered.

Gohtaro was fifty-one years old and a large stocky man,
but Nagare placed a hand lightly on his shoulder as if was
petting the head of a child.

'The guy you came to meet is in the toilet. He'll come back

soon, so rather than getting up like that, you'd be better off waiting.'

Gohtaro became a little calmer. According to the rules, standing up from the chair instantly took you back to the present; if not for Nagare, he would most probably be there now.

'Ah, thank you.'

'No problem,' replied Nagare in rather a clinical manner, and walked away to stand behind the counter with his arms folded. Standing there, he looked less like a waiter and more like a sentry guarding a castle.

No one else was in the cafe.

But there were people in the cafe. On that day twenty-two years ago, there had been a couple sitting at the table closest to the entrance and one person at the counter.

And where Gohtaro was sitting now, in the seat that returns you to the past, there had been a near-elderly gentleman wearing a tuxedo and boasting a well-groomed moustache.

The gentleman's look had seemed very old-fashioned. Gohtaro clearly remembered him because he had thought, *That guy looks like he has time-travelled from the 1920s.*

However, the three other customers had left quickly, perhaps because they could not bear Gohtaro's filthy state or his odd stench.

Then he remembered. As soon as they had entered, Shu-ichi had enthusiastically declared that this was a mysterious cafe where it was possible to go back in time. Then, after listening to his account of what had happened to him, he had gone to the toilet.

Gohtaro wiped sweat from his brow with his palm and drew a deep breath in through his nose. Then, from the back room, a girl of elementary-school age appeared with a brand-new *randoseru* backpack.

'Come on, Mum, hurry!' the girl yelled as she skipped and pranced around the cafe.

'I bet you're happy now, huh?' said young Nagare to the girl circling around in the centre of the cafe, his arms still folded.

'Yeah,' replied the girl with a happy smiling face and she scampered out of the cafe.

CLANG-DONG

Gohtaro had some memory of this happening. At the time, he had not paid much attention, but he was pretty sure a woman who seemed to be the girl's mother would soon emerge and he turned and looked towards the back room.

'Stop, wait for me, please!'

A woman appeared. She had beautiful jet-black hair and a complexion so pale it was almost translucent. Probably in her late twenties, she was wearing a pale peach tunic and a beige frilly skirt.

'Oh, what to do with that child. The new students' welcoming ceremony is not even until tomorrow,' she mumbled, throwing her hands up though not quite in dismay. Her expression revealed joy more than anything as she let out a sigh.

Upon seeing the woman's face, Gohtaro felt startled.

*Could it be?*

He had seen her face before. She totally resembled the woman in the white dress who had been sitting in this very chair reading a novel before he came to the past.

Perhaps they were two different people who just happened to look alike. Human memory is a vague thing, after all. It was someone that he had just been looking at, but his head was confused.

'Are you sure you'll be OK?' asked young Nagare to the woman as he unfolded his arms and squinted. His expression was difficult to read but his tone of voice revealed that he was concerned for her.

'Of course, I'll be fine. We're just going out to look at the cherry blossom in the neighbourhood,' she said reassuringly with a smile and a nod.

Based on the conversation, one would think the woman was in poor health, but from what Gohtaro could see, she didn't appear to be in any discomfort. Having brought up Haruka as a single father, Gohtaro knew all too well about making sacrifices if it would bring a child joy.

'So, thanks for taking care of the cafe, Nagare, it really helps,' said the woman as she moved towards the entrance. She turned to look around one last time, nodded to Gohtaro and left.

CLANG-DONG

As if switching places with the woman, Shuichi Kamiya came back from the toilet.

*Uh . . .*

All thoughts about the woman vanished from Gohtaro's

head the moment Shuichi appeared. The memory of his original mission flooded back.

Shuichi looked like the young man he remembered. Or in other words, he must have looked startlingly old to Shuichi.

'What?'

The Gohtaro that Shuichi had just been talking with had suddenly aged while he was in the toilet. He stared at Gohtaro with a baffled expression.

'Shuichi.'

As Gohtaro spoke, Shuichi held both hands up.

'Wait, wait, wait!' he said, cutting him short. Staring at Gohtaro with hostility, he seemed to freeze like a figure in stop motion.

*This doesn't look good . . .*

Gohtaro had thought Shuichi would surely grasp the situation immediately if suddenly he appeared as his older self – after all, it was Shuichi who told him you could travel back in time in this cafe.

He had grounds for his faith in Shuichi, too.

Perception had always been Shuichi's strong point. When it came to observational skills, an ability to analyse things, and his sense of judgement, Shuichi demonstrated above-average talent. On many occasions Gohtaro had witnessed this being put to good use in Shuichi's seamless plays on the rugby field. Shuichi studied an opponent's character and habits before the match and stored it all in his head. As playmaker, he executed tries perfectly while making fools of the opposing players. No matter how intimidating the situation, he never erred in his analysis or judgement.

Yet it seemed the current circumstances were too impossibly weird and hard to believe, even for him.

While placing both hands around the cup to check its temperature, Gohtaro spoke.

'Shuichi, the truth is . . .'

He was going to explain the current situation, but the cup was cooling faster than he had anticipated. There was simply not enough time to explain things in enough detail to clear everything up. Beads of sweat once again began to gather on his brow.

*What can I tell him?*

He was in a pickle. If he explained everything, the coffee would certainly go cold. If Shuichi didn't believe that he had come from the future, it all would have been for nothing.

*Can I explain it well enough? No, I don't think I can.*

Gohtaro knew he was pretty lousy at explanations. Perhaps if he had lots of time, but he had no idea how long he had left before the coffee cooled. Shuichi was still eyeing him suspiciously – probingly, even, as if his gaze was burning deep into Gohtaro's heart.

'I don't expect you to believe me however much I try to explain, but . . .' Gohtaro began spitting out words, knowing that he had to say something.

'You've come from the future, haven't you?' Shuichi spoke to him very carefully as if he was a stranger who didn't understand the local tongue.

'Yes!' Gohtaro replied loudly, instantly excited by Shuichi's excellent perceptiveness.

Shuichi rubbed his head with his fist, mumbled incoherently and continued his questions.

'From how many years?'

'Huh?'

'From how many years in the future did you come?

Open to the possibility but sceptical at the same time, Shuichi started gathering information. This is exactly what he used to do before a rugby game – put together the necessary information, piece by piece.

*He hasn't changed.*

Confronted by Shuichi's questions, Gohtaro decided to answer them. That would be the fastest way to gain his understanding.

'Twenty-two years.'

'Twenty-two years?'

Shuichi's eyes widened. Gohtaro had never seen him look so surprised, even when he had spotted him living in rags on the street.

Although Shuichi had told Gohtaro about the rumour surrounding this cafe, he never expected to find himself face to face with someone from the future. Also, considering Gohtaro had somehow aged twenty-two years while he was in the toilet, it was little wonder he was surprised.

'You certainly have aged,' mumbled Shuichi, his expression softening a little. It was a sign that he was letting his defences down.

'I guess I have,' replied Gohtaro a little self-consciously.

Here he was, a middle-aged man of fifty-one, acting like a shy child in front of this twenty-nine-year-old. For Gohtaro, he was once again meeting his guardian angel, who had helped him get his life back.

'But you look fit and well, yeah?' said Shuichi, whose eyes were bright red. 'Hey . . . what's up?'

Gohtaro almost got up from his seat, surprised by the look on Shuichi's face. He had imagined that Shuichi would be shocked suddenly to see him old like this, but he hadn't expected a reaction like this.

Shuichi moved closer and keeping his eyes locked on Gohtaro's he sat down opposite him.

'Shuichi?'

The *pit-a-pat* of tears falling could be heard.

Apprehensively and hesitatingly, Gohtaro began to speak, when Shuichi said with a trembling voice, 'Dapper suit you're wearing . . .'

Again, the *pit-a-pat* continued.

'Looks good on you.'

Gohtaro had appeared there in front of Shuichi, the future form of the close friend whose life he was about to turn round. The Gohtaro he had just encountered on the street outside was ragged and forlorn. This was why Shuichi was now experiencing a deep heartfelt joy at the sight of Gohtaro before him.

'Twenty-two years? I bet there were some tough times along the way?'

'Not really, it's flashed by pretty fast . . .'

'Oh?'

'Yeah . . .'

Shuichi, his eyes still red, beamed a broad smile.

'Thanks to you,' Gohtaro said softly to this smiling face.

'I see, *ha*.' Shuichi laughed with embarrassment and

pulled out a handkerchief from his jacket and blew his nose. But the *pit-a-pat* of tears falling on the table continued.

'So, what is it?'

Shuichi stared questioningly at Gohtaro as if to ask, *Why did you come?* He didn't mean it to sound like he was interrogating him. But he knew this cafe's rules, particularly the limit on their time for reunion. He also couldn't imagine Gohtaro coming to see him without reason. So rather than wallowing in sentimentality, Shuichi felt he had no choice but to get straight to the point.

Gohtaro, however, wasn't immediately forthcoming with an answer.

'Are you OK?' Shuichi asked in the same tone one might use to address a crying child.

'To be honest . . .'

As he slowly reached out to check the coffee's temperature, he tentatively began to explain.

'Haruka has decided to get married.'

'. . . uh?'

It must have been a shock even for ever-sharp Shuichi to hear this from Gohtaro. The smile instantly vanished from his face. Perfectly understandable. For Shuichi back in this time, Haruka was just a newborn.

'What . . . what? What does that mean?'

'Er, don't worry, everything's OK,' said Gohtaro in a relaxed tone. He had imagined Shuichi might get agitated during the conversation.

He brought the coffee to his lips and took a sip. He wasn't sure what temperature counted as cold, but it was still clearly warmer than skin temperature.

*It should still be fine.*

He returned the cup to the saucer. He told the story he had prepared beforehand. He did his best to avoid anything that might cause Shuichi to get upset. Most importantly, he had to make sure he didn't say anything that would lead ever-astute Shuichi to suspect that he had died.

'Actually, the future-you asked me to go back in time to get you to give a speech at Haruka's wedding.'

'I wanted to get me?'

'Yeah, like a surprise.'

'Surprise? . . .'

'Future Shuichi and past Shuichi can't meet, you see . . .'

'And so, you came?'

'Yeah, that's right,' continued Gohtaro, growing increasingly impressed with Shuichi's perceptiveness.

'OK, I think I get the idea . . .'

'So, what do you say? It's pretty out there, don't you think?'

'For sure, it's very strange.'

'Yeah, isn't it just.' Gohtaro pulled out a newly bought ultra-slim digital video camera, nothing like what had existed twenty-two years earlier.

'And that is?'

'It's a camera.'

'That tiny thing?'

'Yeah. It records video too.'

'Video too?'

'Yeah.'

'Awesome.'

Shuichi was looking hard into Gohtaro's face as he searched for the on button of the camera he was still not used to.

'It looks like you just bought it.'

'Huh? Er, yeah, that's right.' Gohtaro answered Shuichi's question without much thought.

'You've still got to work on your end game, you know,' Shuichi muttered with a serious face.

'Yeah, sorry, I should have worked out how to use the darn thing before coming,' Gohtaro replied, his ears blushing.

'I'm not talking about the camera,' said Shuichi, maintaining his stern tone.

'Huh?'

'Oh, never mind.'

Shuichi reached out and put his hand on the cup. Familiar with this cafe's rules, he must have been worried about how much time was left.

'Right, let's do it!' he exclaimed. He stood up with a burst of enthusiasm and spun around so that his back was to Gohtaro.

'We've just got a single shot at this, right?' he asked.

Based on the temperature of the coffee, Gohtaro didn't think there would be time to reshoot either.

'Yes. This will be great,' he replied. 'OK then, I'm taking it.' He pressed the record button.

'You know . . . you've always been a terrible liar,' Shuichi muttered.

His words must not have reached Gohtaro, as he didn't seem to react. He simply continued to point the camera at Shuichi.

'To Haruka, twenty-two years from now. Congratulations

on getting married.' Then he grabbed the camera and quickly stepped away from Gohtaro's reach.

'Hey!' Gohtaro yelped and stretched out his hand to get it back.

'Don't move!' Shuichi said.

Gohtaro didn't. Hearing Shuichi's strong tone sent a chill down his spine. If that warning had come a split second later, he would have leaped up from his seat. Luckily he remembered just in time. If he had stood up, he would have been returned to the present immediately.

'What did you do that for?' he asked.

His voice echoed loudly in the room, but luckily they were the only two customers. Aside from them, it was just Nagare behind the counter, and he didn't seem to care about the to-and-fro between them. He stood motionless with his arms crossed, showing not a hint of surprise.

Shuichi let out a deep breath, turned the camera to himself and started talking.

'Haruka. Congrats on getting married.'

Gohtaro still was unclear on Shuichi's motives for taking the camera, but when he saw that he was going ahead and recording a message, he was relieved.

'On the day you were born, the sakura were in full bloom . . . I still remember when I first held you in my arms, how bright red you were, such a tiny thing all curled up.'

Thanking his lucky stars that Shuichi was cooperating, Gohtaro reached out and took the coffee cup, intending to return to the present immediately after Shuichi's message was finished.

'It brought me so much happiness just looking at your

smiling face. Watching you as you slept gave me all the motivation I needed. Being blessed by your birth is the greatest
joy in my life. You are more precious to me than anyone in
the world. If it is for you, I can do anything . . .'

Everything was going to plan. He just needed to get the
camera back and return to the present.

'I wish you have a happy life for as long . . .' Shuichi's voice
suddenly started to crack with emotion. 'For as long as you
live.'

*Pit-a-pat, pit-a-pat.*

'Shuichi?'

'Can we cut the charade?'

'What?'

'Stop lying to me, Gohtaro!'

'Lying? What do you mean?'

Shuichi looked up at the ceiling and sighed heavily. His
eyes were as red as they could get.

'Shuichi?'

Shuichi was biting the back of his hand. He seemed to be
trying to stifle his emotions with pain.

'Shuichi!'

'I . . .'

*Pit-a-pat.*

'Won't be attending . . .'

*Pit-a-pat, pit-a-pat.*

With gnashing of teeth, his words came out bit by bit.

'Haruka's wedding, will I?'

'What do you mean? I said that it was your idea, didn't I?'
Gohtaro urgently spun words together.

'You didn't seriously expect me to be fooled by such lies, did you?' Shuichi retorted.

'They're not lies!'

Upon hearing this, he turned and looked at Gohtaro with his bright red eyes.

'If you're telling the truth, why have you been continually crying all this time?'

'Huh?'

*Pit-a-pat, pit-a-pat.*

*What? I think I'd notice if I was crying,* thought Gohtaro, but it was as Shuichi had said. Huge teardrops were falling from his eyes, and their splashes were making a *pit-a-pat* sound that reverberated around the cafe.

'Oh, that's strange. When did I start doing that?'

'You didn't notice? You've been crying the whole time.'

'The whole time?'

'Ever since I came out from the toilet, you've been crying.'

Gohtaro looked down to see that a puddle of his tears had formed on the table.

'Th-these are ju-just . . .'

'And that's not all, either.'

'Huh?'

'The way you announced, "Haruka's getting married" like that. You spoke of her like a father would of his own daughter. I can't help thinking, you've been raising Haruka like a daughter in place of me!'

'Shuichi . . .'

'Which means . . .'

'No, you've got it wrong.'

'Come on, give it to me straight.'

'. . .'

'So, I'm . . .'

'No . . . Shuichi, wait . . .'

'. . . I'm dead, then?'

*Pit-a-pat, pit-a-pat.*

Instead of answering, Gohtaro's flow of tears surged.

'That's heavy,' muttered Shuichi.

Gohtaro was exaggeratedly shaking his head as a child might, but he couldn't deceive him any longer. Against his will, tears streamed down his face.

His shoulders shuddered as he held back his sobs. To hide his tears he bit down hard on his lip and bowed his head.

Shuichi walked around the room and slumped down into the seat closest to the entrance.

'When?'

Shuichi was asking when he would die.

Gohtaro wanted just to down the coffee and return to the present, but with his fists firmly clenched on his knees, he was frozen stiff, unable even to twitch.

'No more lies . . . OK? . . . Give it to me straight,' pleaded Shuichi looking Gohtaro in the eyes.

Gohtaro looked away and brought his hands together as if praying. He let out a heavy sigh.

'In a year . . .'

'. . . I've just got one year?'

'It was a car crash.'

'Oh god, really?

'You were with Yoko . . .'

'Oh god, no. Yoko too?'

'So, I brought her up. I raised . . . Haruka.'

Gohtaro struggled with how to say Haruka's name without sounding like her father, and Shuichi clearly noticed.

'I see . . .' he muttered with a weak smile.

'But I plan on bringing it to an end . . . today,' said Gohtaro with his voice trailing off.

Gohtaro had never been able to get rid of the thought that the father–daughter relationship that he had built with Haruka over the past twenty-two years had been gained through Shuichi's death. Nevertheless, that spending his days with Haruka brought him happiness was beyond question.

But the happier he felt, the stronger his suspicion that with Shuichi left by the wayside, that happiness was not his to grab . . .

If he had been able to tell Haruka that he was not her real father earlier, perhaps the relationship built between the two of them would be different. But there was no point imagining what might have been.

Haruka's wedding day would soon arrive. Putting it off until he would be revealed by the family register had only intensified his feelings of guilt.

*I have lived my life unable to tell the truth for risk of losing my own happiness.*

That was a betrayal of Shuichi, his guardian angel, and of Haruka.

*I'm so pathetic, I don't deserve to attend something as special as Haruka's wedding.*

And so he had planned to remove himself from Haruka's life after revealing the truth.

Still holding the camera, Shuichi slowly rose. He came to stand beside Gohtaro, who remained slumped. He pointed the camera so that both men were in the shot and he put his arm around Gohtaro's shoulder.

'You're not planning on going to the wedding, are you?' asked Shuichi, shaking Gohtaro's shoulder.

Shuichi had seen through everything.

'No, I'm not,' answered Gohtaro, still hunched over. 'Even though Haruka's father is Shuichi . . . is you . . . I could never tell her about you, her real father. You were the one who helped me . . . and I know I shouldn't have . . . but I thought that if Haruka was my real . . . daughter, then . . .' Gohtaro continued stumbling over his words. 'And I ended up contemplating what should have been unthinkable.'

He brought both hands up to cover his face as he started bawling uncontrollably.

It had been his endless suffering.

By thinking, *What if Haruka was really my own daughter*, it was as if Shuichi had never existed. Gohtaro, whose feelings of indebtedness to him were insurmountable, despised himself for having thought such a thing.

'OK, I get it now . . . and it's just like you to do this to yourself . . . you've been suffering inside your head the entire time, haven't you?'

Shuichi sniffed deeply through his runny nose.

'OK, fine . . . let's finish it today,' he continued, tugging at Gohtaro's earlobe.

'I'm sorry, I'm so sorry . . .' repeated Gohtaro, as tears fell through the crack between his hands still covering his face, and landed *pit-a-pat* on the table.

'Right!' said Shuichi as he pointed the camera to himself.

'Haruka, listen! I have a proposition for you,' he announced. His booming voice reverberated confidently through the cafe.

'Starting from today,' he began, pulling Gohtaro in close by the shoulder, 'your father shall be both me and Gohtaro. Does that sound OK?' he proposed straight into the camera.

Gohtaro's shoulder stopped shaking with sobs. Shuichi didn't pause.

'Starting from today, you get an extra dad. That's quite a bargain. What do you say?'

Gohtaro slowly lifted his teary face.

'Hang on, what are you saying?' he muttered in confusion.

Shuichi turned to Gohtaro.

'You deserve to be happy!' he quipped with utter conviction. 'You can damn well stop tormenting yourself by thinking about me,' he urged.

Gohtaro remembered.

Shuichi had always been like this. It never mattered how tough the going was, he was the eternal optimist. Ploughing on had always been the only the option. And like always, he was being the man who, even after just learning of his own death, could think of the happiness of others.

'Be happy! Gohtaro . . .'

In the corner of the small cafe, two hulking men were hugging each other and crying.

The ceiling fan above them still spun slowly.

Shuichi was first to stop crying. He grabbed Gohtaro's shoulder.

'Hey! Look at the camera. We're making a message for Haruka's wedding, aren't we?'

Gohtaro, supported by Shuichi's arm, was finally able to look into the camera, but his face was puffy and soaked in tears.

'Well, smile then,' Shuichi urged. 'Come on, both of us are going to put on smiley faces and wish Haruka a happy wedding day, aren't we?'

Gohtaro tried to smile, but it was no good.

On seeing Gohtaro's attempt, Shuichi laughed boisterously. '*Ha ha*, nice look,' and he put the camera into Gohtaro's hand.

'You're definitely going to show this to Haruka, OK?'

Upon saying this, Shuichi stood up.

'I'm sorry, Shuichi.'

Gohtaro was still crying.

'Is something wrong with the coffee?' queried Nagare in a low voice from behind the counter. It was his way of expressing concern. The coffee was going cold.

*You're not forgetting the time, are you?* was what he meant.

'Yeah, you should go,' said Shuichi. Gohtaro stared into Shuichi's eyes.

'Shuichi!' he yelled.

'It's OK. Don't worry, I'm OK,' he replied but it did nothing to dispel Gohtaro's gloomy expression. He smiled wryly.

'Hey! Are you planning on attending Haruka's wedding as a spook or something?' he asked, patting Gohtaro on the shoulder.

Gohtaro turned his tear-drenched face towards Shuichi.

'Sorry,' he muttered.

'Hey, it's OK, drink up!' retorted Shuichi, waving his palms.

Gohtaro took the cup in his hands and, feeling that it had pretty much gone cold, gulped it all down in one.

'Uh . . .'

A feeling much like dizziness once again enveloped him.

'Shuichi—!' Gohtaro shouted, but he had already begun to vaporize. His voice didn't seem to have reached Shuichi. Yet, just when he thought his shimmering surroundings would begin to ripple, in his hazy state he clearly heard Shuichi say:

'Look after Haruka for me.'

These were the same words the twenty-two-year younger Gohtaro had heard one year from then, on a day when the snow-like sakura petals had danced across the clear sky.

Gohtaro suddenly found that, just as on the way back in time, the speed with which he was being returned to the future was increasing, he was being propelled along. He lost consciousness.

'Monsieur?'

Gohtaro came to, to the voice of Miki. The cafe interior looked exactly the same. But there before him were Miki, Nagare and Kazu.

*Was it a dream?*

Gohtaro's focus abruptly shifted to his hand and to the camera in it. He hurriedly tried pressing the play button.

As he was looking at the screen, the woman in the dress returned from the toilet and stood in front of the table.

'Move!' she spat out in a frightening, deep, guttural tone.

'Ah, sorry,' Gohtaro said, getting up in a hurry to vacate the seat for her.

The woman in the dress sat down with a nonchalant expression and pushed the cup that remained on the table away from her, obviously an order to clear it away.

The unwanted cup was quickly collected up by Miki. Without the aid of a tray, she carried the cup in both hands. She scuffled past Gohtaro and returned to Nagare's side behind the counter.

She passed the cup to Nagare.

'Monsieur's crying, darlings. *Moi* wonders if he's OK?' she asked, adopting her camp tone once again. Nagare looked over at Gohtaro peering into the camera screen while crying hard enough to make his shoulders shake. The sight must have worried him too. 'Are you OK there?' he asked.

'I'm OK,' Gohtaro answered, glued to the screen.

'Well . . . OK then,' Nagare said, and looked down at Miki. 'He says he's OK,' he whispered. Kazu came out from the kitchen holding a new coffee for the woman in the dress.

'How did it go?' she asked Gohtaro as she stood alongside the special chair, wiped the table and served the coffee.

'Be happy . . .' Gohtaro said softly as he looked towards the chair '. . . is what he said.' He clenched his teeth.

'Oh really?' replied Kazu quietly.

The screen was showing Shuichi with his hand around Gohtaro's shoulder urging him to 'Smile, smile'.

'So OK, darlings, when will *moi* be able to do that?'

Gohtaro had made his way to the cash register and was getting ready to pay. Miki continued to tug at Nagare's T-shirt sleeve.

'Well, first of all, you can quit with the *moi*!'

'But *moi* wants to do i – t.'

'I won't let a person who says *moi* do it.'

'Well, you're just a yellow-belly.'

'I'm just a what?'

While Nagare and Miki continued their stand-off, Gohtaro started to leave but stopped mid-step.

'If I may ask . . .' he said to Kazu, looking at the two.

'Yes?' replied Kazu.

'She was your mother, wasn't she?' Gohtaro asked looking over at the woman in the dress.

Kazu followed Gohtaro's gaze.

'Yes,' she answered.

Gohtaro wanted to ask why her mother hadn't come back from the past. But Kazu was giving off an air that barred any further discussion, her expressionless face still looking at the woman in the dress.

When Gohtaro had asked the same question before going back to the past, Kazu had said that the woman had returned to meet her dead husband.

*That girl has probably suffered far more than I ever have*, thought Gohtaro.

Unable to find any words to express any of that, he said, 'Thank you very much . . .'

And with that, he left the cafe.

### CLANG-DONG

'Twenty-two years ago . . .' Nagare muttered, sighing.

'You must have been just seven years old, right?' he asked from behind the counter, speaking to Kazu, who was looking at Kaname.

'Yes . . .'

'I'm hoping that you too find happiness . . .' Nagare muttered softly as if to himself.

'Well, I—'

Kazu appeared to be about to say something, but Miki didn't wait for her.

'Hey darlings . . . how long before *moi* is allowed to do it?' she asked, becoming entwined in Nagare's legs.

Kazu looked at Miki and smiled warmly.

'Do you ever let up?' asked Nagare, letting out a deep sigh. 'Your time will come!' he said, attempting to untangle himself from Miki wrapped around him.

'When will that be? What time, which day?'

'Your time will come when your time comes!'

'I don't understand,' Miki said, glued to Nagare's leg, refusing to be separated. 'When, when, whe – n?'

Just when Nagare's patience was just about gone . . .

'Miki, your turn will come too . . .' said Kazu, joining the conversation. She moved close to Miki and crouched down so she was at eye level with her.

'When you turn seven . . .' she whispered gently.

'Really?' Miki asked, gawking straight into Kazu's eyes.

'Yes, really,' Kazu confirmed.

Miki looked up at Nagare and waited for his answer.

By his expression, Nagare didn't seem fond of the idea, but in the end, he let out a sigh of resignation.

'OK,' he answered, and nodded a couple of times.

'Yippee, hooray!' Miki was instantly over the moon with joy. She skipped and jumped with everything she had, and scuttled away into the back room.

Shaking his head, muttering, 'What have I gone and said,' he chased after her.

Left behind, Kazu was silently looking at the woman in the dress reading her novel.

'I'm sorry, Mum, I still . . .' she suddenly whispered.

The ticking of the three wall clocks reverberated loudly as if in tune with Kazu.

Always . . . . . .

Always . . . . . .

# II

*Mother and Son*

---

Nothing makes you think, *Ah, autumn has arrived,* more than hearing the *chirp-chirp* of the *suzumushi*, the bell cricket.

Such warm feeling towards insects, however, is a unique cultural phenomenon. Beyond Japan and Polynesia, the chirping of insects tends to be described as a complete racket.

According to one theory, both the Japanese and Polynesian peoples originally travelled south from Mongolia. The phonetics of Samoan, one Polynesian language, are similar to Japanese. Both have vowels comprising the five tones of 'a', 'i', 'u', 'e', and 'o', and the words of both languages are expressed using consonants and vowels, or vowels alone.

Japanese also has onomatopoeic expressions to communicate sounds, and mimetic expressions to convey states that do not produce sounds. But whether it's the onomatopoeic *sala-sala* sloshing of the flowing river and the *byuu-byuu* blowing of the wind, or the mimetic *shin-shin* to describe the quiet settling snow and *kan-kan* that expresses the beating down of the sun's rays, all these words evoke the mood of the world around us.

These words come alive in the Japanese comics of today, where they appear directly over the illustrations outside the caption bubbles. When a character strikes a dramatic pose, *ZUBAAN!* is added for emphasis, or *DOHN!* is added to intensify the crashing of a heavy object. *Sulu-sulu* adds texture to a slippery surface, and the quality of silence is encapsulated by *shi – n*. When these comics use glyphs in this way, it heightens the reality of the moment.

There is a song often sung in school music classes that is full of these expressions.

> *I can hear the pine cricket chirp!*
> *Chin-chillo chin-chillo chin-chillo-lin*
> *I can hear the bell cricket chirp!*
> *Lin-lin lin-lin li – n-lin.*

One autumn evening . . .

Miki Tokita was singing this song, 'Harmony of the Insects', in a loud spirited voice. She was keen for her father, Nagare Tokita, to listen to the song she had learned at school that day. And all her singing was making her face quite red.

Nagare was struggling to continue to listen to Miki's out-of-key and very loud notes. A deep furrow was forming in the middle of his forehead, and his mouth was fast resembling an upside-down 'U'.

'*Chirping throughout the long autumn night.*
*Oh, what fun to hear this insect symphony!*'

When she finished singing, Miki was met with applause.

'Wonderful, wonderful,' said Kyoko Kijima, clapping her hands. Kyoko's praise left her smiling with a smug sense of achievement.

'*I can hear the pine cricket . . .*' she started singing again.

'All right, Miki. Very nice, but enough!' said Nagare, desperate to stop her song. Having heard it three times already, he was well and truly sick of it. 'Thank you for sharing your song, now go and put your *randoseru* away,' he said, picking up her school bag from the counter and holding it out to her.

Miki, still gloating from Kyoko's praise, said, 'OK,' and disappeared into the back room.

'*Chin-chillo chin-chillo chin-chillo-lin . . .*'

Just as the singing Miki left the room, the cafe's waitress Kazu Tokita appeared. 'Well, it certainly feels like autumn has arrived,' she muttered to Kyoko. Miki's singing had apparently heralded autumn's arrival in the cafe, which always looked the same, regardless of the season.

**CLANG-DONG**

Entering the cafe as the bell rang out was Kiyoshi Manda, a homicide detective at Kanda Police Station who was around sixty. It was early October, and the mornings were beginning to get quite chilly. Kiyoshi removed his trench coat and sat down at the table closest to the entrance.

'Hello, welcome,' said Kazu as she served him a glass of water.

'Coffee, please,' Kiyoshi replied.

'Coming straight up,' Nagare said from behind the counter, and popped into the kitchen.

When Nagare had gone, Kyoko whispered so that only Kazu could hear, 'Kazu, the other day, I saw you walking in the front of the station with a man! Who was that? You don't have a boyfriend, do you?'

Smiling mischievously with a playful sparkle in her eyes, Kyoko was no doubt waiting for Kazu to react in some way rarely seen – to blush, or something similar.

But she simply looked Kyoko in the face and replied, 'Yes, I do.'

Kyoko looked genuinely surprised.

'Really? I didn't know you had a boyfriend!' she bellowed, leaning closer to Kazu standing behind the counter.

'Well, I do.'

'When did this happen?'

'He was a senior student while I was at art school.'

'You mean you've been dating for ten years?'

'Oh, no. We've been dating since spring.'

'Spring this year?'

'Yes.'

'Oh, really?' mused Kyoko, leaning back in her seat until she was precariously close to losing her balance. She let out an enormous sigh.

Of the people in the cafe, however, Kyoko was the only one revelling in the surprise. Kiyoshi didn't appear to have any interest in such gossip. His was only concerned with the black notebook in his hands, which he was staring at, deep in thought.

Kyoko yelled into the kitchen, where Nagare was.

'Hey, Nagare! Did you know Kazu has a boyfriend?' It was only a small cafe. After shouting, Kyoko looked at Kazu and shrugged, *Maybe that was too loud?* and checked Kazu's face for signs of embarrassment.

Kazu, however, calm as always, was polishing a glass. In her mind, there was nothing to hide. She was simply answering because she was asked.

As there was no reply from Nagare, Kyoko once again called out, 'Well, did you?' After a moment, a reply came.

'Yeah, sort of, I guess.'

Strangely, Nagare appeared far more evasive and bashful than Kazu.

'Well, I'll be!'

As Kyoko, once again, turned to stare at Kazu, Nagare came out from the kitchen.

'Why is it such a surprise?' Nagare asked Kyoko. He walked over and served Kiyoshi the freshly brewed coffee.

Kiyoshi looked pleased, and smiling broadly, he slowly inhaled over the cup.

Upon observing this, Nagare's narrow eyes arched in pleasure. That the coffee he served in the cafe was never just ordinary was a source of great pride and joy to him. Getting to see Kiyoshi's smile was his reward. He puffed out his chest with an air of satisfaction and returned behind the counter.

Caring not one iota about Nagare's sense of satisfaction, Kyoko went on.

'I suppose I shouldn't be, but you know, it's Kazu. Who would have thought she had a secret romantic life.'

'Uh-huh,' Nagare replied with indifference, further narrowing his eyes. He started humming a tune while polishing a silver tray. In terms of importance, it seemed Kiyoshi's smiling face far outweighed such talk of Kazu's boyfriend.

Kyoko looked sideways at Nagare.

'So, what were you doing that day?' she asked Kazu, probingly.

'We were looking for a present.'

'A present?'

'It was his mother's birthday.'

'I see, I see.'

And so, for a little while, Kyoko continued to probe and dig with various questions about Kazu's boyfriend. Kyoko asked about Kazu's first impressions of him when they met, about how he went about asking her out, and so on. As Kazu was willing to answer anything Kyoko threw at her, the questions never ended.

Of everything she asked, Kyoko seemed most interested in the number of times that he had asked her to be his girl-friend. Rather than it being a one-off, he had done it three times: soon after they met, three years after that, and lastly, in spring this year. Kazu had been willing to answer all of Kyoko's questions. But as to why she had refused him twice but said yes on the third time, she replied with a vague 'I don't know.'

When she finally ran out of questions, Kyoko rested her cheeks on her hands and asked Nagare for another coffee.

'So why has the simple news that she has a boyfriend put you in such a good mood?' Nagare asked as he poured her a refill.

Kyoko replied with a beaming smile. 'My mother, you see, was always saying that she wished the day when Kazu was happily married would arrive soon.'

Kyoko was referring to her mother Kinuyo, who had

passed away the previous month after a long battle with illness.

Kinuyo, who had taught Kazu art since she was a young girl, loved Nagare's coffee. Right up until she was admitted to the local hospital, she was a regular customer who visited the cafe whenever she had time. Both Kazu and Nagare were incredibly fond of her.

'Oh, was she?' Nagare mused solemnly. Kazu made no comment, but her hands had stopped polishing the glass she was holding.

Sensing she had brought everyone down, Kyoko added in a hurry, 'Oh, stupid me, sorry for ruining the atmosphere. I didn't mean to suggest Mum had died with unfulfilled wishes. Please don't take it the wrong way.' But Kazu of course knew that Kyoko hadn't meant it like that.

'On the contrary, thank you,' Kazu replied with a gentle smile that she ordinarily didn't show.

Kyoko felt she had dampened the mood, but she seemed pleased to have had the chance to share Kinuyo's wishes with Kazu. 'Oh, my pleasure,' she replied with a happy nod.

'Excuse me, if I might interrupt . . .'

It was Kiyoshi. He had been quietly sipping his coffee, obviously waiting for a break in the conversation.

'There is something I would like to ask . . .' he said with a terribly apologetic expression.

Who he had directed this question to was unclear, but Kyoko replied instantly, 'Yes?' as did Nagare with, 'What is it?' And Kazu, rather than responding, simply looked directly at Kiyoshi. Removing his shabby hunting cap, Kiyoshi scratched his head of mostly white hair.

'Actually, I'm struggling to come up with an idea for what to buy my wife for her birthday,' he muttered, sounding a little embarrassed.

'A present for your wife?' asked Nagare.

'Yes.' Kiyoshi nodded. Perhaps, on hearing the conversation about Kazu choosing a present for her boyfriend's mother, he had thought that he might learn something useful.

'Aww, how romantic,' Kyoko said teasingly, but Kazu took the question more seriously.

'What present did you get her last year?' she asked.

Kiyoshi again scratched his head of white hair.

'Well, I'm embarrassed to admit it, but I've never actually bought my wife a birthday present. So, I don't know what to buy her.'

'What? You've never bought her anything? But even so, you suddenly want to now . . . Why's that?' Kyoko asked with wide-eyed curiosity.

'Oh, I don't know, there's no particular reason . . .' he replied, pretending to take another sip from the coffee cup he had clearly emptied. Kyoko could, as plain as day, see through his attempt to conceal his embarrassment. She desperately tried to hide her spontaneous chuckle, giving away how adorable she found it.

Nagare had been standing with his arms crossed, listening to the conversation. 'How I see it . . .' he muttered, then went on enthusiastically, his face completely red, '. . . is that she would be pleased with anything.'

Kyoko was quick to dismiss his suggestion. 'That would have to be the least helpful advice you could give him!'

Feeling well and truly put in his place, Nagare conceded,

'Er, sorry.' Then Kazu, with the coffee flask in her hand, refilled Kiyoshi's cup.

'What about a necklace?' she asked.

'A necklace?'

'It isn't the flashiest of things . . .' As she spoke Kazu showed her necklace to Kiyoshi. It was so thin, it hadn't even been noticeable until she held it in her fingers.

'Which? Show me. Oh, yes! Very nice! Women have a weakness for that type of thing at whatever age,' said Kyoko, peering at Kazu's neckline and nodding emphatically.

'By the way, how old are you now, Kazu?' asked Kiyoshi.

'I'm twenty-nine.'

'. . . Twenty-nine,' Kiyoshi muttered as if thinking something over.

Noticing Kiyoshi's expression, Kyoko sought to reassure him. 'If you are worried whether it is age-appropriate, don't worry! It's a wonderful gesture. I think your wife would be pleased with such a gift.'

Kiyoshi's face brightened instantly.

'I see. Thank you very much.'

'Happy shopping.'

Kyoko was both surprised and impressed. She never would have guessed that a ham-fisted ageing detective like Kiyoshi would be planning a birthday present for his wife. She was fully committed to supporting him in this endeavour.

'Yes, thank you,' Kiyoshi replied, returning his shabby hunting cap to his head and reaching again for his cup.

Kazu was also smiling happily.

*'I can hear the lion roar!*

*Roar-roar, roar-roar ROOAAAARRR! Roar!'*

The sound of Miki's singing drifted from the back room.

'I don't remember that verse,' observed Kyoko with her arms folded as she stared into space.

'It seems to be her latest thing.'

'What, replacing the lyrics?'

'Uh-huh.'

'Now that I think about it, kids love doing that, don't they? When Yohsuke was Miki's age, it didn't matter where we were, you wouldn't believe what he would swap lyrics with, I remember it being so embarrassing.'

Smiling nostalgically, Kyoko looked towards the back room where Miki was.

'Speaking of Yohsuke, he hasn't been coming in with you lately,' Nagare remarked, changing the subject.

Yohsuke was Kyoko's son. He was in grade four at elementary school and a regular football nut. While Kinuyo was still in hospital, Kyoko and Yohsuke had often come to the cafe together, to take one of Nagare's coffees to her.

'Huh?'

'Yohsuke.'

'Ah . . . yeah,' Kyoko muttered, reaching for her glass.

'He only came because Mum asked for coffee,' she explained and downed the remaining water.

Yohsuke had stopped coming to the cafe immediately after Kinuyo had died. After a six-month battle with illness, Kinuyo had wet her mouth with a coffee brewed by Nagare and taken her last breath as if falling asleep.

When Kinuyo passed away, the non-coffee-drinking elementary-school-aged Yohsuke no longer had a reason to come.

At the end of summer, six months after Kinuyo had first been hospitalized, Kyoko had said that she was 'preparing herself'. But one month had passed since her mother's death, and she was unable to disguise the grief in her expression.

Nagare hadn't meant Yohsuke's not coming to the cafe to lead to the subject of Kinuyo's death, and he seemed to be regretting bringing it up.

'Ah. Sorry to mention it,' he said bowing his head slightly. Then suddenly . . .

*'I can hear the cockerel crow!*

*Cock-a-doodle cock-a-doodle COOCCKK-A-COCKOH!'*

Miki's energetic singing could be heard from the back room.

'Pmph!' Kyoko erupted at Miki's alternative lyrics. The serious atmosphere she had created transformed instantly. *Saved by Miki*, she probably thought. Kyoko let out a raucous laugh.

'I think she just crossed a cockerel with a bush warbler, though,' she said looking at Nagare. He seemed to be thinking the same.

'Hey, Miki, you're starting to sing some pretty odd lyrics!' he said, and, sighing heavily, he headed off to the back room.

'Miki can be so cute sometimes,' Kyoko muttered to herself.

'Well, I must be going . . . thank you for the coffee,' said Kiyoshi, taking advantage of the change in atmosphere. He carried his bill to the cash register where he pulled out some change from his coin purse and placed it on the tray, nodding politely.

'Thanks for the wonderful advice today, it really helped,' he said, and with that, he left.

## CLANG-DONG

Only Kyoko and Kazu remained in the cafe.

'And how's Yukio getting along?' asked Kazu softly as she picked up the coins from the tray and pressed the clunky keys on the cash register. Yukio was Kyoko's younger brother. He was living in Kyoto, training to become a potter. Surprised that she had raised the topic of Yukio, for a moment Kyoko just stared wide-eyed at Kazu. Kazu simply maintained her usual detached expression and poured some water into Kyoko's empty glass.

*Kazu sees everything.*

Kyoko sighed, realizing that she would have to explain.

'Yukio didn't know Mum was in hospital. She wouldn't let me tell him . . .'

Kyoko reached out for the glass of water, lifted it few centimetres off the counter, but rather than bringing it to her lips, she slowly swirled it.

'So, I think maybe he's angry about that? He didn't even come to the funeral.'

Kyoko's gaze was concentrated on the surface of the water, which remained level even as she tilted the glass at various angles.

'I think his phone's been disconnected . . .'

In fact, Kyoko hadn't been able to get in contact with Yukio at all. She rang his phone, but only heard 'The number you have dialled is currently not being used' – the announcement that is given when the account has been cancelled. She had tried contacting the pottery studio where he was working, but they said he had quit a few days earlier, and no one knew his whereabouts.

'I have no idea where he is right now . . .'

For the last month, Kyoko hadn't been able to stop thinking about how Yukio hadn't known that Kinuyo was in hospital (if it had been her who was kept in the dark, she would have been beside herself with anger, and who knows what she might have said or done). It had been troubling her so much, she hadn't been able to sleep properly for days.

There was the rumour that this cafe allowed customers to go back in time. Kyoko, of course, had laid eyes on customers who had rolled up wanting to return to the past. But she had never thought that something might happen to make her want to go back to put things right.

There was a 'but', however. She wanted to set things right, but she knew all too well that she couldn't. The reason was that even if she were to travel back, there was the rule that *no matter how hard you try while back in the past, present reality cannot be changed.*

Hypothetically, even if she returned to the day Kinuyo was hospitalized and wrote a letter to Yukio, the principle of this rule would prevent any letter she sent from being delivered to him. Even if that letter were delivered, for some reason, he would never read it. As a result, he would suddenly learn of Kinuyo's passing without even having known that she had been hospitalized. Furious, he would not make an appearance at her funeral. Because that is how the rule works. And if she couldn't change reality, there was no point returning to the past.

'I really understand Mum's feelings about not wanting to cause Yukio any worry . . .'

But it was precisely this reasoning that put Kyoko in the double bind that now caused her such distress.

'But . . .'

Kyoko covered her face with both hands and her shoulders started to quake. Kazu stuck to the job of waitress, and without much call for her services right now, time flowed by silently.

*I can see Daddy coming along!*

*Poot-poot poot-poot farty bug*

*Chirping throughout the long autumn night.*

*Oh, what fun to hear this insect symphony!'*

Miki's odd alternative lyrics could be heard coming from the back room. But this time, Kyoko's laughter did not echo through the cafe.

That evening . . .

Kazu was alone in the cafe. Well, strictly speaking, both Kazu and the woman in the dress were there. Kazu was tidying up, and the woman in the dress was, as usual, quietly reading her novel. She seemed to be nearing the end. She was now holding down only a few unread pages with her left hand.

Kazu enjoyed this time in the cafe after it was closed. It wasn't because she particularly liked tidying up or cleaning, she simply enjoyed completing a task in silence without thinking about anything. This was the same enjoyment she felt when drawing.

In her art, Kazu was particularly skilled at using a pencil to draw something she could see in front of her in photo-realistic detail. She enjoyed the technique known as hyper-realism. She didn't just draw anything, however. If it was something visible in the real world, she would draw it. But she never drew from her imagination and nor did she draw anything that couldn't exist. Also, her drawings always excluded subjective feeling. She simply enjoyed the process of depicting what she saw on a canvas without thinking about anything.

*Flap!*

The sound of the woman in the dress shutting the book having finished it reverberated throughout the cafe.

The woman placed the novel in one corner of the table and reached her hand to the coffee cup. Spying this, Kazu pulled out a novel from under the counter and approached the woman.

'This one probably won't be completely to your taste . . .' Kazu said as she placed the book in front of the woman and collected the one left on the table.

She had carried out this action over and over, so often that each movement was done with procedural swiftness. But while she did, her usual cool expression was temporarily replaced by the look of someone about to pass a carefully chosen present to a special someone with the hope that it will bring them joy. When people choose presents hoping to delight the recipient, they have in mind that special person's reaction. And as they do, they often find that time has suddenly got away from them.

The woman in the dress was not a particularly fast reader. Despite it being the only thing she did, she would finish a book about once every two days. Kazu would go to the library once a week and borrow a selection of novels. These books weren't presents, exactly, but for Kazu, supplying them was more than just a 'task'.

Until a couple of years ago, the woman in the dress read a novel entitled *Lovers*, over and over again. One day, Miki remarked, 'Doesn't she get bored reading the same novel?' and presented her own picture book to the woman in the dress. Kazu thought, *What if I could please her with a novel I chose? . . .* and that's what led her to start providing novels in this way.

As always, however, without a care for Kazu's thoughtfulness, the woman in the dress simply reached out, took the book silently and dropped her eyes to the first page.

The expectation disappeared from Kazu's expression like sand silently falling in an hourglass.

### CLANG-DONG

The doorbell rang, which was unusual because it was past closing time and the 'Closed' sign hung from the door. But Kazu didn't worry about who it could be. Instead, she casually returned behind the counter and looked towards the entrance. The person who came in was a man with a tanned complexion who might be in his late thirties. Over a black V-neck shirt, he wore a dark brown jacket. His trousers were a similar colour, and his shoes were black. He glanced around the cafe vaguely, with a dull, melancholy expression.

'Hello, welcome', Kazu greeted him.

'Er, it seems you're closed now?' he enquired tentatively. That the cafe was indeed closed was obvious.

'I don't mind', Kazu replied, gesturing for him to take a seat at the counter. He sat down as suggested. He seemed exhausted, and his movements were sluggish, as if in slow motion.

'Would you like a drink?'

'Um, no . . .'

Normally if a customer came into a cafe after closing and then didn't want to order anything, it would be disgruntling to a waitress. But Kazu simply accepted the man's reply without hesitation. 'OK.' She quietly served him a glass of water.

'Er . . .' The man seemed to realize his behaviour was a bit strange and grew agitated. 'Sorry. On second thoughts, I would like a coffee please.'

'Certainly', replied Kazu, averting her eyes politely, and she disappeared into the kitchen.

The man gave a deep sigh and looked around the sepia-coloured cafe. He noticed the dim lamps, the ceiling fan gently rotating, the large clocks on the wall showing seemingly random times, and the woman in the white dress reading a novel in the corner.

Kazu returned.

'Um . . . Is it true that she is a ghost?' the man enquired abruptly.

'Yes.'

The man had asked a very strange question. But Kazu had

answered it matter-of-factly. Many customers came to the cafe out of sheer curiosity after hearing its legend. Kazu had grown so used to such conversations that now they were like small talk for her.

'I see . . .' replied the man, sounding uninterested.

Kazu started to prepare the coffee in front of him. Ordin-arily, she used the siphon. The special feature about coffee brewed by siphon is that boiling hot water in the bottom flask noisily bubbles and rises to the funnel, where it becomes coffee. Then the liquid drops back down into the top flask. Kazu enjoyed watching the siphon brewing in action.

However, for some reason, today she didn't choose to use the siphon but instead brought the drip-coffee equipment from the kitchen. She brought the mill out with her as well, obviously planning to grind the beans at the counter.

The brewing method of using the dripper was the cafe owner Nagare's speciality. The filter is set in the dripper and hot water is gently poured over the grounds to extract the coffee bit by bit. Kazu normally thought the dripper was too much trouble.

She silently proceeded to grind the beans. There was no conversation. Revealing himself to be far from outgoing, the man just scratched his head, seemingly unable to strike up any kind of exchange. Soon, the aroma of coffee began to fill the air.

'Sorry for the wait.'

Kazu placed the lightly steaming coffee in front of the man.

He remained still, just staring at the cup in silence. Kazu began cleaning the apparatus in front of her deftly.

The only sound in the room was the woman in the dress turning the pages of her novel. After a while, the man reached his hand out for the cup. If he had been a coffee-loving customer, at that point he would have inhaled the aroma deeply, but without altering his dull expression, he sipped the coffee with a clumsy slurp. But then . . .

'This coffee,' he moaned quietly. Its sourness seemed to have surprised him. His expression transformed as furrowed lines formed in the centre of his forehead.

The coffee was a variety called mocha, which has a unique blend of pleasant aroma and acid-sour taste. Nagare was obsessed with this taste, and the cafe only served varieties of mocha. However, for people who normally don't drink coffee, like this man, the strong distinctive flavour of coffee brewed from only mocha or Kilimanjaro beans is often bewildering.

The names of coffee beans mostly derive from where they are grown. In the case of mocha, the beans are grown in Yemen and Ethiopia and named after Yemen's port city of Mocha, where they were traditionally shipped from. Kilimanjaro beans are grown in Tanzania. Nagare enjoyed using beans grown in Ethiopia, and there were certain people who loved their strong acid-sour taste.

'It is mocha Harrar. It was Kinuyo sensei's favourite.'

Upon hearing this suddenly from Kazu, the man gave an involuntary start and looked at her with open hostility.

Of course it wasn't the name of the coffee that had surprised him; it was the waitress, who he had never met before, mentioning Kinuyo's name even though he hadn't even told her his.

His name was Yukio Mita, the aspiring potter, Kinuyo's son, and Kyoko's younger brother. Although Kinuyo had been a long-time regular, Yukio had never visited the cafe before. Kyoko, who lived a relatively close fifteen-minute drive away, had started frequenting the cafe after coming to buy coffee when Kinuyo was hospitalized. Yukio eyed Kazu with suspicion, but Kazu was not taken aback in the slightest. That she had been waiting for him was unspoken but made obvious by her silent smile.

'When . . .' began Yukio, scratching his head, 'did you know I was her son?' He hadn't purposely set out to conceal his identity, but it seemed to bother him.

Kazu went on cleaning the coffee mill.

'I could just tell. You have a similar face,' she explained.

Not sure how to react to that, Yukio touched his face with his hand. It didn't seem to be something he had been told before, and he looked unconvinced.

'It might be a coincidence, but I saw Kyoko today, and our conversation turned to you. So, it was partly intuition, but I thought it might be you . . .'

Upon hearing Kazu's explanation, Yukio replied, 'Oh, I see . . .' For a moment, he averted his eyes.

'Pleased to meet you. I'm Yukio Mita.' He introduced himself with a nod.

Kazu returned a soft nod of her own. 'Kazu Tokita. Pleased to meet you,' she replied.

'Mum mentioned you in letters. And she wrote about this cafe's rumour as well . . .' Yukio muttered on hearing Kazu's name. He glanced over at the woman in the dress.

He cleared his throat and stood up from the counter.

'I would like to return to the past, please. I want to go back to when my mother was still alive,' he declared with a slight nod.

As a child, Yukio was a serious type who would always persevere with a single task. If he was told to do a job, he would never give up, even when left unsupervised. While on cleaning duties at elementary school, for example, he would carry on with his assigned task even if everyone else was just messing around.

He had a warm personality and treated everyone kindly. Because he associated with the quiet kids in his class all through elementary school, junior high and high school, he never stood out as a student. As a child, he was like dull wallpaper.

Dull Yukio had his epiphany in high school while on a field trip to Kyoto. His assignment was to experience Kyoto's traditional crafts. He had chosen pottery out of pottery, hand fans, seals or bamboo work. Even though it was his first time turning a wheel, the piece of pottery that he created was shaped far better than those of the other students. The pottery teacher told him, 'I've never seen a piece of pottery turned so beautifully by kids in this class. You've got talent!' These were the first words of praise that Yukio had ever received.

The field trip left him with a vague yearning to be a potter, though he had no idea how to go about becoming one. This aspiration persisted, even long after returning from the field trip.

Then one day, while watching TV, he saw a studio potter by the name of Yamagishi Katsura. 'I've been making pottery for forty years now, and I am finally satisfied with what I am making,' the potter said. Looking at the pieces that were shown, Yukio was profoundly moved. It wasn't that he was dissatisfied with his ordinary life, it was just that from somewhere in his heart he heard, *I want to find work that is worth spending a lifetime on.* Yamagishi Katsura was someone Yukio could admire and aspire to become.

There were two different paths he could choose to become a studio potter: one was training at a fine arts university or ceramic arts school, the other was becoming an apprentice at a potter's studio.

Rather than going to a ceramic arts school, Yukio decided to become an apprentice under Yamagishi Katsura. Yukio had liked what Katsura had said on TV. 'To become top class, you must be in touch with top class.' However, when he spoke to his father Seiichi about wanting to be a studio potter, he was told, 'Of the thousands or tens of thousands of people with such an aspiration, only a handful of talented individuals truly put food on the table as a potter, and I don't see that talent in you.' Despite his father's opposition, Yukio didn't give up. He was acutely aware, though, that if he went to university or a ceramic arts school, his parents would have to pay for his tuition.

He didn't want his selfish pursuits to be a burden to his parents, so he decided to train to be a potter while living and working at a studio. Seiichi was against the idea, but in the end, it was Kinuyo who persuaded him, and immediately after graduating from high school, Yukio moved to Kyoto. The studio he chose was, of course, Katsura's.

The day he left for Kyoto, Kinuyo and Kyoko waved him off from the Shinkansen platform. Kinuyo said, 'It's not much but . . .' and handed him her own bank account passbook and ID stamp. Yukio knew that Kinuyo had been diligently saving that money, saying, *Someday, I'd like to travel overseas with your father.*

'I can't take that,' he insisted. But she would not take no for an answer. 'Take it. It's no problem, really.'

The Shinkansen bell rang, and Yukio had no choice but to accept the stamp and passbook with a small nod, and he departed for Kyoto. Left standing on the platform, Kyoko said, 'Mum, let's go now.' But Kinuyo stood on the platform looking at the diminishing train until it disappeared.

'You cannot change the present while in the past, no matter how hard you try, OK?'

Kazu had started to explain the never-changing rules. It was particularly important to emphasize that rule when meeting a person who was now dead. Bereavement is thrust upon people suddenly. Having to process the loss of Kinuyo was especially sudden for Yukio as no one had even told him she had been hospitalized. But Kazu's words left his expression unaltered.

'Yes, I know,' he replied.

Kinuyo's cancer was discovered in spring that year. It was already advanced by the time she was diagnosed, and she was told she had just six months to live. The doctor told Kyoko that had they found it three months earlier, there might have been something they could have done. Because of the rule that said you can't change the present, though, even if Yukio returned to the past to make them discover it earlier, it would not change the fact of Kinuyo dying.

Kazu assumed that Yukio must have heard a bit about the cafe from Kinuyo, but asked, 'Should I briefly explain this cafe's rules?'

Yukio thought for a moment. With a soft voice he replied, 'Yes, please.'

Kazu stopped cleaning and began to explain.

'First, the only people who you can meet while in the past are those who have visited the cafe.'

Yukio replied, 'OK.'

If the person who the customer wants to meet has only visited the cafe once, or if they have shown their face for only a short while before leaving, then the chances of being able to meet them grow slimmer. But in the case of a regular customer like Kinuyo, the chance of meeting her was very high. Considering it was Kinuyo that Yukio was aiming to meet, Kazu didn't feel the need to elaborate further and moved on.

'The second is the rule I mentioned earlier. No matter how hard you try, there is nothing you can do while in the past that will change the present.'

Yukio had no questions regarding this one either.

'OK, I understand,' he answered readily.

'Which brings us to the third rule. In order to go back to the past, you must sit in that seat, the one she is sitting in . . .'

Kazu looked directly at the woman in the dress. Yukio followed her gaze.

'The only time you can sit there is when she goes to the toilet.'

'When will she do that?'

'No one knows . . . But she always does so once a day . . .'

'So, I guess I just have to wait?'

'Exactly.'

'I see,' Yukio replied with a stony face.

Kazu was herself a person of few words, but Yukio also offered few questions or remarks. The explanation was going quickly. 'The fourth rule is that while in the past, you must stay in that seat and never move from it. If you lift your bottom from the chair, you will be forcibly returned to the present.'

If a customer forgets this rule, he or she will face the unhappy consequence of immediately being returned to the present, wasting the chance to go back in time.

'Next is the fifth rule. Your time in the past only lasts from when the coffee is poured to when it goes cold.'

Kazu reached out and took Yukio's glass, which he had emptied at some point during her explanation. Yukio certainly seemed thirsty, as he took frequent sips.

The annoying rules did not stop there.

The journey through time can only be attempted once and once only.

It is possible to take photos.

Presents can be given and received.

Even if you find some way to retain the coffee's heat, it will have no effect and it will get cold anyway.

In addition, in a magazine feature on urban legends, the cafe was made famous as 'the cafe where you could travel back in time', but technically, you could travel to the future too. However, hardly anyone wants to travel to the future, the reason being that although you can travel forwards to exactly where you want to go, you can never be sure that the person you want to meet will be there. After all, no one knows what will be going on in the future.

Other than utter desperation, there is no reason even to bother, as the chances of travelling to the future and happening to meet someone in the narrow window of time until the coffee goes cold are slim. The journey will most likely be futile.

Kazu did not, however, explain all of this. She generally only explained five rules. If asked about the others, she provided answers.

Yukio took a sip of his newly poured water. 'I heard from my mother that if you don't drink all the coffee before it goes cold, you turn into a ghost. Is that true?' he asked, looking directly into Kazu's eyes.

'Yes, that's true,' Kazu replied matter-of-factly.

Yukio averted his gaze and inhaled deeply. 'So, in other words, you die . . . is that what you are saying?' he asked, as if he was just making sure.

No one had ever asked for clarification that becoming a ghost equated to death before.

Until then, Kazu had been able to answer any question without changing her expression. But for that moment only, her expression faltered. And it truly was only for a moment. After letting out a shallow breath, in the time it took for her eyelashes to flutter a couple of times she adopted her usual cool persona again.

'Yes, that is correct,' she replied.

Yukio nodded, appearing somehow satisfied with her answer. 'Right, OK,' he muttered as if he understood.

Upon finishing explaining the list of rules, Kazu looked over at the woman in the dress.

'Now all you need to do is to wait for her to leave her seat. Do you plan on waiting?' she asked. It was her final question to confirm whether Yukio was really going to go through with visiting the past. He did not hesitate.

'Yes,' he replied. He reached for the coffee cup. The coffee must have been cold by now but he drank it in one gulp. Kazu reached out and took the empty cup.

'Would you like a refill?' she asked.

'No, I'm fine,' he said, with a wave of refusal. The coffee that Kinuyo had enjoyed drinking every day didn't suit his taste buds.

Halfway to the kitchen, carrying Yukio's empty cup, Kazu stopped in her tracks.

'Why didn't you go to the funeral?' she asked with her back to him.

From the point of view of a son who had not attended his mother's funeral, it could easily have sounded liked an accusation. It was unusual for Kazu to ask such a question.

Yukio frowned slightly, as if he had indeed taken it that way.

'Do I have to answer that question?' he asked, his tone somewhat terse.

'No,' Kazu replied with her cool-as-ever look. 'It's just that Kyoko believes it is her fault that you didn't go to the

funeral . . .' She nodded her head politely and disappeared
into the kitchen.

In truth, it wasn't Kyoko's fault that Yukio hadn't gone to the
funeral. He had certainly struggled with denial when told of
Kinuyo's death, but the bigger reason was he couldn't afford
the fare from Kyoto to Tokyo. When he was notified of
Kinuyo's death, he owed a lot of money.

Three years ago, Yukio, still in training to become a potter,
received an offer for funding if he opened a studio. To own
a studio is every aspiring potter's dream. Naturally, he longed
to have his own studio in Kyoto someday. The offer of funding came from the owner of a wholesale company, newly
established in Kyoto, which bought from the potter Yukio
was working for.

In the seventeen years since he'd left Tokyo, he had been
living in a bathroom-less ten-square-metre apartment to
save money. Without any luxuries, he was simply focused on
his dream.

His overriding motivation was to realize his goal of
becoming a studio potter quickly, so that he could show
Kinuyo. Upon reaching his late thirties, his impatience had
only grown. Accepting the offer, he borrowed the rest of the
money from a personal finance company, gave it to the
wholesale company owner along with all his savings, and
proceeded to prepare to open his studio. All did not end well,
however, as the owner of the wholesale company ran off with
the money that Yukio had entrusted to him.

He had been cheated, and the result was devastating. Not only did he still not have his pottery studio, but he was now also in enormous debt. It felt like he had fallen into a deep crevasse of financial hell from which he didn't think he could escape. It was mental torture.

Every day, worry over making repayments overwhelmed his brain, leaving no room for other things, like the future. The only thing he could think of was, *How can I raise the money? What can I do tomorrow to raise the money . . .?*

*Would I be better off dead?*

Many times, this thought entered his mind. But if he died, the burden of repayment would fall to his mother, Kinuyo, and that was something he wanted to avoid at any cost. That possibility alone stood between him and his desperate thoughts of suicide.

This precarious tension was what Yukio was going through when one month earlier he learned of her death. At the news, he heard a tautly stretched string snapping inside his head.

When Kazu was out of sight, Yukio calmly plucked his mobile phone from his jacket pocket, checked the screen and sighed in annoyance.

'No signal . . .' he muttered, looking over at the woman in the dress. A moment later, his eyes shone as if he had suddenly thought of something. He stood up and, quickly assessing that the woman in the dress was not going to the toilet just yet, briskly left the cafe.

### CLANG-DONG

The bell rang, and soon after . . .

*Flap!*

The sound of the woman's novel shutting resonated throughout the room. Perhaps Yukio had just left his seat to ring someone, but it was such terrible timing. The woman in the dress tucked her novel under her arm, silently rose from her seat and began walking towards the toilet.

The cafe had a large wooden door at the entrance. On the right was the toilet. Walking slowly, the woman in the dress passed through the entrance arch and turned right.

*Clunk.*

Just after the toilet door closed softly, Kazu entered the empty room from the kitchen.

Yukio was missing. If it had been Nagare in Kazu's shoes at this moment, he would have searched for him frantically. Now was the time – the once-daily chance to travel back in time. But it was Kazu.

Far from growing frantic, she stayed completely cool as if the customer's absence was no big deal. She started clearing away the woman in the dress's used cup, behaving as if Yukio had never existed. She didn't seem to have the slightest interest in why he had gone out or whether he was coming back. She wiped the table with a cloth and then disappeared back into the kitchen to wash the cup. The doorbell rang.

### CLANG-DONG

Yukio re-entered the room empty-handed, his mobile phone now stowed in his pocket. He sat down at the counter, which meant his back was to the chair. Lifting the glass in front of him, he sipped his water and exhaled a deep sigh, unaware the woman in the dress was gone.

Kazu appeared from the kitchen carrying a silver kettle and a bright white coffee cup upon a tray. Noticing Kazu, Yukio said, 'I just contacted my sister,' explaining why he had left his seat. His voice no longer sounded as defensive as it had when he had responded to Kazu's question about why he didn't attend the funeral.

'Oh, really?' Kazu replied quietly.

Yukio looked up at Kazu standing there and gulped. She seemed to be haloed by dim pale blue flames, and he sensed an unworldly and mysterious atmosphere hanging in the room.

'The chair's vacant . . .' began Kazu.

He finally noticed that the woman in the dress was no longer there and gasped, 'Ah!'

Walking up to the now unoccupied chair, Kazu asked him, 'Will you be sitting down?'

Yukio stared vacantly for a moment, as if still shocked that he had not noticed the woman's absence. But conscious of Kazu's patient gaze, with some effort he replied, 'Yeah, I will.'

He walked over, silently closed his eyes, and after taking a deep breath, he slid between the table and the chair.

Kazu placed the pure white cup in front of him.

'I shall now pour the coffee,' she said softly. Her calm voice had a sombre gravitas.

'The time you can spend in the past will begin from the time the cup is filled, and it must end before the coffee gets cold . . .'

Although she had explained this rule to him earlier, Yukio didn't immediately respond. After closing his eyes as if deep in thought, 'OK, I understand,' he replied, more to himself than to Kazu. His voice sounded different now, its pitch ever so subtly lower.

Kazu nodded, and she picked up from the tray a ten-centimetre-long silver implement that looked like a stirring stick and slipped it into the cup.

Yukio looked at it curiously. 'What's that?' he asked, cocking his head to one side.

'Please use this instead of a spoon,' she explained simply.

*Why doesn't she just give me a spoon?* he wondered. But he was conscious that listening to the explanation alone was taking up valuable time.

'OK, got it,' he merely replied.

Having finished her explanation, Kazu asked, 'Shall we begin?'

'Yes,' Yukio answered. He downed his glass of water and took a deep breath.

'Let's begin now, please,' he added softly.

Kazu nodded and slowly lifted the silver kettle in her right hand.

'Pass on my regards to Kinuyo sensei,' she said and added . . .

'Remember, before the coffee gets cold . . .'

Moving as if in slow motion, Kazu began pouring the coffee into the cup. While still maintaining a casual demeanour, her movements were beautiful, flowing seamlessly like those of a ballerina. The entire cafe around them seemed pregnant with tension, as if a solemn ceremony was underway.

A very thin column of coffee poured from the silver kettle's spout, resembling a narrow black line. There was no gurgling sound of coffee pouring as one might hear from the wide rim of a carafe. Instead, the coffee flowed silently into the brilliant white cup. As Yukio stared at the striking contrast of black coffee and white cup, a single plume of steam began to rise. Just at that moment, his surroundings began to shimmer and ripple.

In a panic, he tried to rub both his eyes but found he was unable to. As he lifted his hands to his face, they still felt like hands, but they were now vapour. It wasn't just his hands, it was his body, his legs – all of him.

*What's going on?*

At first, he was shocked by the unexpected events, but after considering what would follow, nothing seemed to matter any more. He slowly closed his eyes as his surroundings gradually began falling past him.

Yukio remembered Kinuyo.

As a child, he had as many as three brushes with death. On each of these occasions Kinuyo was by his side.

The first time was when he was two. A bout of pneumonia had given him a fever of nearly forty degrees and a persistent cough. Nowadays, pneumonia is no longer difficult to recover from. Thanks to medical advances, there are now effective antibiotics that will knock it on the head. Today, it is common medical knowledge that the main causes of pneumonia for young children are bacteria, viruses, and mycoplasma, and there are clear methods of treatment for each.

Back then, however, it was not uncommon for a doctor to simply say, 'There is nothing else I can do. Now it's up to your son.' In Yukio's case, they didn't know that his pneumonia was bacterial, and when his high fever and severe coughing continued, the doctor said, 'Hope for the best and prepare for the worst.'

The second time he almost drowned. He had been playing at the river's edge when he was seven. Miraculously, on that occasion, he was revived after both his breathing and heart had stopped. The person who found him had fortuitously worked for the local fire and ambulance station and had the ability to administer life-saving CPR immediately. Kinuyo had been at the river with him, but it all happened in a second she had taken her eyes off him.

The third time was a road accident when he was ten. While riding his brand-new bike, he was rammed by a car that had ignored the traffic lights. The impact sent him flying right in front of Kinuyo's eyes. He was thrown almost ten metres and had to be carted off in an ambulance with multiple injuries to his whole body. He was on the brink of death but luckily his head was unscathed, and he miraculously regained consciousness.

Parents can't prevent their child getting ill, being injured, or having an accident. On all three occasions, Kinuyo nursed him without sleep or rest until he recovered. Apart from toilet breaks, she never left his side, holding his hand in both of hers as if she were praying. Her husband and parents were worried that she would burn herself out and urged her to rest, but she wouldn't listen. A parent's love for their child is bottomless. Their children remain children, no matter how old they grow. For Kinuyo, that feeling never changed, even when Yukio left home on his quest to become a celebrated potter.

He had become an apprentice to that famous potter. He received free food and board at the potter's house, but it was agreed that he would work without pay. So, after spending the day at the pottery studio, he would earn some money by working at a convenience store, or places like an *izakaya* bar at night. He could easily cope with that kind of lifestyle in his twenties, but in his thirties it became physically gruelling. He started receiving a small wage from the pottery studio, but, unable to stand sharing a room for ever, he rented an apartment, which immediately made life much harder.

Despite all this, he always put a little away so that he might own his own pottery studio in the future. Kinuyo would occasionally send a box of instant foods along with a letter, and this helped supplement his meals.

Some weeks he had as little as one thousand yen to spend. Everyone else his age had a proper job and was doing things that adults did, like falling in love and buying new cars. But Yukio was in front of the kiln getting covered in smoke and soot. He would knead his clay and dream of the day when he would be an acclaimed potter with his own studio.

There were many times when he felt like giving up, filled with doubt about his talent. He was in his thirties and couldn't see how he could go on working in casual jobs. If he wanted to find something decent, he had better quit soon – in this difficult job climate, no company was going to hire him after forty. Even now, he would find it hard. How much longer could he go on like this?

How long would it take him to become a successful potter with his own studio? He felt uneasy about how uncertain his future was. His was a life with no guarantees. With marriage out of the question, each day for him was a battle with the clay.

Yet he still clung to that thin strand of hope that he would fulfil his dream and make his mother proud. As long as he felt that there was someone who would find joy in his success, that was enough for him. Even if he was mocked and laughed at by society, at least he knew that Kinuyo believed in his success.

But . . . never in his worst nightmare had he imagined being swindled out of every penny and then falling into massive debt.

The news of Kinuyo's death reached him when he was at his lowest – just when he needed someone's support the most. It sent him plummeting into the depths of despair. Why this cruel timing? Why was he plagued by such bad luck?

What had all his efforts been for, what had he been living for, all this time? Maurice Maeterlinck's book *The Blue Bird* told a similar story. The main characters, the children, Tyltyl and Mytyl, encounter a child in the 'Kingdom of the Future' who is destined to bring into this world nothing except three illnesses. This child would catch scarlet fever, whooping cough and measles soon after birth, and die. Yukio remembered the sadness he felt when reading this book as a child. If that kind of fate was unalterable, then how unfair life was! If people didn't have the power to alter their undeserved fate, then he just couldn't see their reasons for living.

When Yukio came to, his eyes were flooded. He only realized they were tears when he wiped away those that ran down his cheeks with his hands. His hands, once vapour, had returned to the corporeal world, and his surroundings, which had been flickering past him, had at some point stopped moving.

*Whirr, whirr-whirr . . .*

Hearing the sound of grinding coffee beans, he looked around at the counter. The rotating ceiling fan, the shaded lamps, the large wall clocks – none of these had changed from several seconds earlier. But the person behind the counter was different. Yukio had never laid eyes on this giant with almond-shaped eyes who was doing the grinding. Only Yukio and the giant were present in the room. Immediately, he was gripped by doubt.

*Have I really returned to the past?*

He couldn't think how to make sure. Certainly, Kazu the waitress was no longer there, and there was a giant he didn't know behind the counter. His body had turned to vapour, and he had seen his surroundings flowing past him. That alone, however, was not enough to convince him that he had travelled back.

The man behind the counter stood casually grinding beans, unfazed by Yukio's appearance. Even though Yukio was a stranger to him, and he had suddenly appeared in this chair, he seemed to be acting as if it was all perfectly normal. He didn't even show any interest in talking to him, which suited Yukio fine. He was in no mood to come to this place and answer a flurry of questions. But he did want to know whether he had returned, as he had wished, to a time when Kinuyo was alive.

Kyoko had said that Kinuyo was hospitalized six months earlier, in spring. He needed to ask what month and year it was.

'Er . . .' he began before being interrupted . . .

CLANG-DONG

'Hello.'

The layout of the cafe meant that there was a moment, straight after the doorbell rang, when you didn't know who had entered. But Yukio knew whose voice it was immediately.

*Mum . . .*

After a few moments of watching the entrance near the cash register, he saw Kinuyo hobble in, using Yohsuke's shoulder for support.

'Ah . . .'

The moment he saw Kinuyo, he turned his face away so that she would not see him. He bit his lip.

*Have I come just before she was hospitalized?*

The last time he had seen Kinuyo in the flesh was five

years earlier. At that time, she was still fit and well. She hadn't needed someone's shoulder to help her walk. But appearing before him now, she had withered terribly. Her eyes were sunken and white hairs covered her head. Her hand gripped by Yohsuke had bulbous veins, and each finger looked like a thin cane. Already, her illness had wasted her body.

*She is so frail! I had no idea . . .*

His face was frozen as it was, unable to look up.

The first to notice him was Yohsuke.

'Grandma . . .'

Yohsuke spoke softly into Kinuyo's ear as he slowly helped her turn towards Yukio. Grandma's boy, Yohsuke had become her hands and feet, and he knew how to support her frailness.

When she saw it was Yukio at whom Yohsuke was looking, her eyes widened.

'Oh goodness . . .' she said softly.

Responding to her voice, Yukio finally looked up.

'You look well!' he said.

His voice was brighter than the one he had spoken to Kazu with.

'What's up? Why are you here?'

Kinuyo seemed very surprised that Yukio, who was meant to be in Kyoto, had suddenly made an appearance in this cafe. But her eyes were shining joyfully.

'There's a little something,' he said, returning a smile.

Kinuyo whispered in Yohsuke's ear, 'Thank you,' and walked by herself to the table where Yukio was seated.

'Nagare, one coffee for me if you please. I'll drink it here,' she requested politely.

'One coffee coming up,' Nagare replied. Before she had even asked, he had already put the beans he had just ground in the filter. He only had to pour over the steaming hot water, and the coffee would be made.

Since Kinuyo always came to the cafe at the same time, he had ground the beans to coincide with her arrival. Yohsuke plonked himself down on a counter seat facing Nagare.

'And what is young Yohsuke going to have?'

'Orange juice.'

'Orange juice it is.'

After taking Yohsuke's order, Nagare took the pot and began pouring the hot water over the grounds in the filter holder that was in the shape of the letter 'e'.

The aromatic fragrance of the coffee began to drift through the cafe. Kinuyo's elated grin made it clear how much she loved this moment. She exhaled a noisy 'Oof!' as she sat down in the chair facing Yukio.

Kinuyo had been a regular at this cafe for decades. So, naturally she knew the rules well. It must be clear to her by now, without needing to be told, that he had come from the future. Yukio wanted desperately to avoid telling her the reason he'd come.

*I came to see my dead mother . . .*

There was no way to say those words. He hastily felt the need to say something.

'You look like you've lost weight.'

As soon as he blurted it out, he was cursing himself for saying such a thing.

He didn't know whether she had been diagnosed with cancer, but it was the period leading up to her hospitalization – of course she was thin. Turning the topic of conversation to her illness was the very thing he'd wanted to avoid. A pool of sweat was forming inside his clenched fists.

But Kinuyo simply replied, 'Oh, really? That's nice to hear.' Placing both hands on her cheeks, she looked happy to hear it. On seeing her reaction, he thought, *Perhaps she still doesn't know that she has cancer.*

Sometimes people don't find out until they are in hospital. Her reaction was completely understandable if she didn't know about her illness. This came to Yukio as a relief.

He relaxed a little. He tried his best to keep the conversation casual and normal.

'Really? You're happy to hear me say that, even now?' he laughed dismissively. But Kinuyo's expression was earnest.

'Yes, I am,' she replied. 'You're looking pretty thin, yourself,' she added.

'. . . Oh, you think?'

'Are you eating properly?'

'Yeah, of course. Recently I've even been making my own meals.'

Yukio hadn't eaten one proper meal since he'd heard of her death.

'Oh, really?'

'Yeah, rest assured, Mum, I've given up living on cup noodles.'

'What about washing your clothes?'

'Sure, I'm washing my clothes.'

He had been wearing the same clothes for nearly a month.

'No matter how tired you are, you must always make the effort to sleep on a futon.'

'Yeah, I know that.'

He had already cancelled the lease on his apartment.

'If you get into money trouble, don't borrow from people. Speak up about it, OK? I don't have much myself, but I can give a little.'

'Money is fine . . .'

Yesterday, he finished filing for personal bankruptcy. There would be no burdening Kinuyo and Kyoko with massive debt.

Yukio simply wanted to see Kinuyo's face one last time.

If it was possible to change the present by going back in time, then he probably wouldn't have chosen this ending. He would have done everything possible to ensure his mother, sitting in front of him, could get the best hospital treatment. He would have explained the circumstances to that large man he didn't know behind the counter and begged him to take some action.

The reality was, however, that none of his wishes would come true. His life had lost all meaning. Not wanting to break Kinuyo's heart was his only grip on life. That single powerful feeling inside him kept him going, despite having been cheated into a life of endless hardship. He had resolved not to die while his mother was still alive.

But back in the present, Kinuyo was no longer there . . .

His face was at peace as he spoke to her.

'I'm able to open my own studio now. I'm going independent as a potter.'

'Really?'

'Yeah, I'm not lying.'

'How wonderful.'

Tears began spilling from Kinuyo's eyes.

'Hey, that's not something to cry about,' he said, handing her a paper napkin.

'It's just . . .' No more words came from her.

While looking at Kinuyo's teary face, Yukio calmly pulled out something from inside his jacket.

'So, anyway, here . . .' he said, placing it before her. It was the passbook and stamp that she had given him when he first left for Kyoto.

'I thought I would need it if things got hard, but I ended up not using it . . .'

No matter how tough life had become, he could never bring himself to use the money. It was filled with the wishes of his mother, who – never doubting his success – had believed in him as she sent him off. He was planning to return it to her when he succeeded as a potter.

'But that money . . .'

'No, it's OK. Just knowing it was there enabled me to get through the hard times, no matter how tough things got. It gave me the strength to keep going. I always ploughed on so that I could return it to you, Mum.' That was not a lie. 'Please, I want you to take it.'

'Oh, Yukio . . .'

'Thank you.' He nodded deeply.

Kinuyo took the passbook and stamp from him and held them to her chest.

*Well, that's the last burden gone. Now I just have to wait for the coffee to get cold.*

Yukio had never intended to return to the present.

Since hearing of Kinuyo's death, he had thought only of this moment. He couldn't just die. If he left debt, it would cause trouble for his family.

For the last month, he had frantically been preparing for personal bankruptcy. Although he didn't even have the money for the bus or train fare to get to the funeral, he worked as a labourer every day until he had enough to hire a lawyer and to pay to travel to the cafe. It was all for this moment.

As if all the taut lines holding him together had come undone, his body felt completely drained of strength. Not having slept properly for the last month might also have been a factor. His fatigue had reached its limit. Now, everything would end.

*Finally.*

He felt satisfaction . . .

*Now, it's all much easier.*

. . . and a sense of having been released.

When suddenly . . .

*Bip-bip-bip-bip bip-bip-bip-bip* . . .

A softly beeping alarm sound was coming from his cup. He didn't know the purpose of this alarm but when he heard it, he remembered Kazu's words. He pulled the beeping stirrer from the cup.

'That reminds me, the waitress here said to pass on her

regards . . .' He conveyed to Kinuyo the words Kazu entrusted him with.

'You mean Kazu?'

'Um, yeah.'

'Oh . . .'

Kinuyo's expression darkened for a brief moment. But then she closed her eyes and inhaled deeply, and quickly looked at Yukio directly again with a smile.

'Er, Kinuyo . . .' Nagare called out from behind the counter.

Kinuyo looked back at him. Smiling broadly, she simply said, 'I know.'

Mystified at this exchange, Yukio reached out for the cup and took a sip.

'Hmm, that's nice,' he lied. The strongly acidic sour taste was not to his liking.

Kinuyo looked at him with gentle eyes. 'She is such a kind girl, isn't she?'

'Huh, who?'

'Kazu, silly.'

'Kazu? Oh, yes, for sure.'

Yukio lied again. He had no room in his head to consider Kazu's personality.

'She really sees people's true feelings. She always thinks about the person who sits in that chair.'

Yukio had no inkling of what Kinuyo was trying to say. But as he was planning to sit it out until the coffee went cold, it didn't matter what she talked about.

'There was a woman in the white dress sitting in that chair, right?'

'A woman? Oh, yes, yes there was.'

'She went back to see her late husband, but she never returned . . .'

'Oh, really?'

'No one knows what exchange took place. But even so, no one ever considered that she might never return.'

Yukio noticed that behind the counter Nagare was standing slumped with his head hung low.

'It was Kazu who poured the coffee for her. She had only just turned seven.'

'. . . Oh, really,' Yukio muttered, seemingly uninterested. He didn't get why Kinuyo wanted to tell him this now.

Her face was sad as she heard his reply.

'To think, your own mother, of all people!' she said with a slightly sterner tone.

'Huh?'

'The woman who didn't return was Kazu's mother!'

The change in his complexion suggested that even Yukio was moved by these words.

It was such a cruel turn of events for a young girl, who still needed her mother's love, to go through. Just imagining it was painful. But while it stirred some empathy in him, it didn't make him feel any more like returning to the future.

He wondered how this conversation and the stirrer were connected.

He began considering the question clinically.

Kinuyo picked up the stirrer from the saucer.

'So, you see, ever since then, Kazu places this in the cup of anyone who goes back to visit someone who has died,' she explained while waving it. 'It rings before the coffee gets cold.'

'. . . Oh.'

Yukio's face turned pale.

*But that would mean that . . .*

'That was why Kazu sent her regards.'

*She was practically telling Mum that she would die.*

'What? Why did she do that? What right does she have to tell you that? How would that make you feel?'

Yukio still didn't understand the reason for Kazu's action.

*It was none of her business!*

An angry expression clearly formed on Yukio's face.

Kinuyo, however, remained calm.

'What Kazu did . . .' she explained softly, with a very happy smile that Yukio had never seen before – she certainly showed no trace of fear, or any other emotion that one might expect having been told of her death through Kazu's message, 'was to assign me a final task: one that only I can do.'

Yukio remembered that when Kinuyo talked about the times he had nearly died, she used to say with tears in her eyes, 'I wasn't able to do anything for you.' Whether it was illness or accident, she could never forget the torment of waiting helplessly.

'It's time you returned to the future . . .' Kinuyo said kindly with a smile.

'No, I don't want to.'

'Do it for me. I believe in you.'

'No.'

Yukio shook his head dramatically.

Kinuyo held the passbook and stamp he had given her against her forehead.

'I will keep this. It's filled with your wishes. I'll take it to my grave without using it,' she said, bowing her head very deeply.

### CLANG-DONG

'Mum . . .'

Kinuyo lifted up her head and looked at Yukio with a kind smile.

'There is no greater suffering than that of a parent who is unable to save their own child who wants to die.'

Yukio's lips began to tremble.

'. . . Sorry.'

'That's OK.'

'Forgive me.'

'Well now . . .' she said, pushing the cup, ever so slightly, to him. 'Could you say thank you to Kazu for me?'

He tried to say *OK*, but no words came out. He swallowed and grabbed the cup with trembling hands. He lifted his head to see with his now-blurry vision Kinuyo beaming at him, also weeping.

*My sweet boy . . .*

Her voice was too soft for him to hear, but that's what her lips whispered. As if speaking to a newborn.

For a parent, a child is a child for ever. Never ever expecting anything in return, she was simply a mother who wanted her child to be happy, always, to shower him with love.

Yukio had thought that if he died, everything would be over. He thought that it would have no effect on Kinuyo because she was already dead. But he had been wrong. Even after she died, she was still his mother. The feelings did not change.

*I would have upset my dead mother . . .*

Yukio gulped down the coffee. The acidic sour taste

unique to mocha filled his mouth. The dizziness returned, and his body began to turn to vapour.

'Mum!' he yelled.

He could no longer tell if his voice was carrying to Kinuyo. But her voice reached him clearly.

'Thank you for coming to see me . . .'

Yukio's surroundings began to flow past him. Time began to move from the past to the future.

*. . . If the alarm hadn't rung at that moment . . . and I had waited until the coffee went cold, I would have broken Mum's heart at the very end . . .*

His dream was to become a potter with his own studio. He had endured many long years without recognition, held captive by the dream of success. Then he'd been cheated and fallen into a deep despair, unable to see why only his life was so unhappy. But he had been about to cause his mother even greater suffering than he had experienced . . .

*OK, I'll live . . . . . . no matter what happens . . . . . .*

*I'll live for my mother who never stopped wishing for my happiness, right until the very end . . .*

Yukio's consciousness gradually faded as he was transported through time.

When he came to, Kazu was the only other person in the cafe. He had returned to the present. A few seconds later, the woman in the dress returned from the toilet. Silently, she slid up close to him, and looked down at him with a scowl.

'Move!'

Still sniffling, he slowly relinquished the seat to the woman in the dress. She sat down without a word, pushed away the cup that Yukio had used and then proceeded to read her novel as if nothing had happened.

*The entire cafe appears to be glowing.*

Yukio was beset by a mysterious feeling. The lighting hadn't got any brighter. Yet everything now looked fresh to his eyes. His despair at life had metamorphosed into hope. His outlook had changed unrecognizably.

*The world hasn't changed, I have . . .*

Staring at the woman in the dress, he mused over what he had just experienced. Kazu cleaned away his cup and served a new coffee to the woman in the dress.

'Kazu . . .' he called out towards Kazu's back, 'Mum said to say thanks.'

'Oh, did she?'

'Yeah, and I should thank you too . . .'

Upon saying this, he bowed his head very deeply. Kazu walked off into the kitchen to wash up the cup that he had used. When she was out of sight, he slowly took out his hand-kerchief to wipe his tear-soaked face and blow his nose.

'How much is it?' he called to Kazu. She promptly came out and started reading the bill out loud at the cash register.

'One coffee plus the after-hours surcharge. That comes to four hundred and twenty yen, please,' she replied, pressing the heavy keys of the cash register, her deadpan expression not faltering. The woman in the dress continued reading her novel as if nothing had happened.

'All right then . . . here you are.'

He passed her a thousand-yen note.

'Why didn't you tell me about the alarm?' he asked.

Kazu took his money, and once again pressed the clunky keys.

'Oh, I'm sorry, I must have forgotten to explain that to you,' she replied with a cool expression, bowing her head a little. Yukio smiled, looking genuinely happy.

*Lin-lin lin-lin li – n-lin . . .*

The chirping of a bell cricket could be heard coming from somewhere.

As if egged on by the chirping, Yukio began speaking as Kazu placed the change into his palm. 'Kazu . . . Mum said she hopes you find happiness too,' he said, and promptly left the cafe.

They weren't the words that he had heard from Kinuyo. But considering Kazu's circumstances, he could easily imagine her saying such a thing.


### CLANG-DONG


With Yukio gone, Kazu and the woman in the dress were alone. The doorbell was still softly humming. Kazu took a cloth and began to wipe the counter top.

'*Chirping throughout the long autumn night.*

*Oh, what fun to hear this insect symphony!*'

Kazu sang to herself softly. As if in response, *lin-lin li – n-lin*, chirped the bell cricket.

The quiet autumn night wore slowly on . . .

# III

*The Lovers*

---

A man from the past was sitting in *that chair*.

Not only could you go back in time in this cafe, you could also visit the future. Compared with the number of people who choose to return to the past, however, hardly anyone chooses to venture into the future. Why? Well, whereas you can return to the past and aim to coincide with the person you want to meet, this is simply not possible when heading to the future. The prospects of meeting a particular person at the cafe at a specific time in the future are riddled with uncertainty.

For example, even if you set a date, all kinds of things could happen to hinder that person's journey to the cafe that day. Their train might simply be delayed. There might be an urgent request from work; a road might be closed; a typhoon might hit; the person might be ill – the point is, no one knows what obstacles are waiting. The chances, therefore, of a person travelling to the future and successfully meeting the right person are extremely low.

Yet, there in the cafe, was a man who had come from the past. His name was Katsuki Kurata. He was in knee-length shorts and a T-shirt with beach sandals on his feet. The cafe, in contrast, was decorated with an artificial Christmas tree that reached nearly to the ceiling. It took pride of place in the centre of the room; the middle table had been moved in order to make room for it in this tiny nine-customer cafe. The tree had been bought by Nagare Tokita's wife, Kei, before she died, as a sign of her affection for her beloved daughter Miki (she wanted to leave behind something that could be decorated every year).

Today was 25 December, Christmas Day.

'You're not cold, dressed like that?' asked Kyoko Kijima, who was sitting alongside Miki at the counter. She was half concerned, half amused at how unsuitable Kurata's attire was for Christmastime.

'How about a blanket or something?' suggested Nagare, popping his head out of the kitchen, but Kurata replied, with a quick wave of his hand, 'I'm fine. I don't feel cold at all. But could I have glass of cold water please?'

'OK, one cold water coming up,' said Kazu Tokita behind the counter. As she spoke, she spun round, pulled a glass from the shelf, filled it with water and walked briskly over to Kurata.

'Thank you,' he said, taking the water from her, and drinking it down all in one go.

'I've finished!' exclaimed a gleeful Miki, gripping a pen. Sitting at the counter next to Kyoko, she had just finished writing a wish on a vertically-folded piece of paper known as *tanzaku*.

As Miki held up the paper, Kyoko asked, 'What did you wish for this time?' while trying to peek.

'I wish that Daddy's feet would start smelling nice,' Miki read out energetically. Finding that terribly amusing, Kyoko blew a short raspberry. Giggling also, Miki dropped down from the seat, and walked over to hang her *tanzaku* wish with the other decorations on the Christmas tree. It was an unusual time to be writing *tanzaku* – something people would normally do on the seventh of July when the Tanabata Festival is held. The tree was already festooned with several such wishes she had written, and their contents varied. Nagare was by far the most common theme among them. Aside from 'smelly feet', she wished that he would 'become shorter' and that he would 'stop being so cranky'. Kyoko often had to suppress her laughter.

Writing wishes on *tanzaku* and hanging them on the Christmas tree was not a regular activity at the cafe. On seeing Miki practising her writing, Kyoko had suggested, 'Why not write wishes and decorate the tree with them?'

Kazu, who normally didn't laugh that much, was chuckling too. The cheerful atmosphere even made Kurata, the man from the past, smile.

'Stop just writing silly things,' an exasperated Nagare grumbled as he came out from the kitchen holding a square twenty-centimetre box. The box held the Christmas cake, made by him, that Kyoko had ordered.

Miki looked at him and giggled, then turned to the *tanzaku* hanging from the tree, clapped her hands and prayed in the traditional Shinto way. Was it Christmas, or the Tanabata Festival, or was she pretending to visit a shrine? It was all very confused.

'Right, next one . . .' said Miki, far from finished, as she began to write once more.

'Oh, not again . . .' Nagare sighed.

After putting the cake box in a paper carrier bag, he said, 'This is for Kinuyo . . .' and added a takeaway coffee in a smaller paper bag.

'Huh?' Kyoko started. Her mother Kinuyo, who died that year in the last days of summer, had always enjoyed drinking Nagare's coffee – she had gone on drinking it every day while in the hospital too.

'Thank you,' Kyoko said softly, tears in her eyes. She was moved by his thoughtful kindness in adding the coffee that Kinuyo had loved, even though she never ordered it.

Bereavement.

It's a part of life, and carrying out acts of mourning allows us not to forget. Perhaps in the case of the large Christmas tree that Kei had left, the tree embodied not only her wish to never be forgotten but was also a sign that she would always be watching over them. As for the way the Christmas tree was used, well, it was unconventional. But if Miki enjoyed it, it was certainly being used in accordance with Kei's wish.

'How much was it again?' asked Kyoko, wiping a tear.

Nagare narrowed his eyes further, perhaps in embarrassment. 'Er, two thousand, three hundred and sixty yen,' he replied softly.

Kyoko pulled the money out of her purse. 'Here you go,'

she said, handing him a five-thousand-yen note and three hundred and sixty yen in change.

Nagare took the money and pressed the clunky keys of the cash register.

'By the way,' he said, then paused. 'He's moving back to Tokyo, isn't he? What's his name, Yukio, was it?' he asked Kyoko. Yukio was Kyoko's younger brother, who had moved to Kyoto to become a studio potter.

'Yes, he's coming home! Things were pretty hard for a while, but he's found himself a job.'

It hadn't been easy for Yukio to find proper work. He had spent his adult years up until his late thirties solely focused on ceramics, leaving him with no qualifications. He was open to any field of work, so he sought help from Hello-Work, the public employment placement service. After eleven unsuccessful applications, he was hired by a small company that sold Western-style tableware. Newly arrived in Tokyo, he chose to live in a company apartment. In this way, he took the first steps towards beginning a second life.

'Oh, that's wonderful to hear,' said Nagare as he handed Kyoko the change. Kazu, who was listening in on the conversation behind Nagare, also bowed her head. Kyoko's expression, however, darkened a little. She looked over at the man in *that chair* and let out a small sigh.

'It never crossed my mind that Yukio was thinking about suicide . . .' she lamented. 'I'm really so grateful,' she said, bowing her head deeply.

'Don't mention it,' said Kazu. Her deadpan expression did not change, so it was difficult for Kyoko to know how well she had conveyed her feelings. Nevertheless, Kyoko nodded, seemingly satisfied.

'I've done another one!' exclaimed a boisterous Miki, who had finished writing another wish.

'Oh, have you? What's the wish?' asked Kyoko with a smile.

'That Daddy becomes happy.' Miki read it out loudly, and then giggled.

It was unclear how deeply she had thought about her wish. She might have just wanted an excuse to write the characters for 'happy'. But on hearing it, Nagare looked almost embarrassed.

'What nonsense!' he grumbled and then promptly vanished into the kitchen. Kyoko looked at Kazu and chuckled.

'I think Daddy is saying he is happy already,' she told Miki and left the cafe. Miki was smiling, but perhaps she hadn't noticed the depth of the feelings she had roused.

### CLANG-DONG

Miki cheerfully attached the *tanzaku* to the tree while singing a Christmas song, as the noisy bleating of Nagare blowing his nose droned on in the kitchen.

'Have you written it?' Miki asked the man in the chair.

She walked up to him and peeked at what was on the table. Placed in front of his hands were a pen and a *tanzaku*, the same materials that Miki had been using. Miki had given them to him so that he could write a wish too.

'Er, sorry, no. I . . .'

'You know you can write anything, OK?' Miki advised

Kurata, who hurriedly grabbed the pen. He looked up at the rotating ceiling fan, as if taking time to think, and then quickly wrote his wish.

'Shall we try to contact Fumiko again?' asked Nagare coming out from the kitchen, his nose red from blowing.

Fumiko was a customer who had returned to the past in this very cafe seven years ago. She still visited often.

'She's not the sort of person to break a promise.' Nagare sighed, crossing his arms. He had tried calling her phone a few minutes earlier, and although it rang, she hadn't answered.

'Thank you, I appreciate you going out of your way,' Kurata said to him, with a polite nod.

'Are you waiting for Fumiko?' asked Miki, who, at some point, had sat herself down facing Kurata and was now studying his face.

'Er, no not Ms Kiyokawa . . .'

'Who's Ms Kiyokawa?'

'Kiyokawa is her surname . . . er, you know what a surname is?'

'I know what a surname is. You mean her last name, right?'

'Yes, that's right! Well done! What a smart girl!'

Kurata was praising Miki as if she had answered correctly in a test. She looked pleased and made a peace sign.

'But Fumiko's last name is Takaga, isn't it? It's Fumiko Takaga, right?' Miki asked Kazu behind the counter. Kazu smiled warmly, but Nagare was quick to correct her.

'It's Ka-Ta-Da! She'll get cross if you call her Fumiko Takaga, OK?' he interjected.

Miki didn't seem to be able to tell the difference between

'Takaga' and 'Katada'. She just tilted her head with a confused expression as if to say, *What is Daddy talking about?*

'. . . Oh, that's amazing news!' Kurata gasped, instantly recognizing the name Katada. Just the mention of it caused him to sit up excitedly. For a moment it looked dangerously like he was about to stand up from the chair in excitement.

'So, she did end up getting married!'

'U-huh, yeah.'

'Oh wow! How brilliant!'

Kurata had heard that Fumiko's now-husband had postponed the wedding after a job opportunity came up in Germany. On hearing the news that she finally did get married, he seemed so delighted that you would think he was the one getting married.

Fumiko's decision to travel back in time had been the result of an unfortunate conversation between her and her then boyfriend, Goro Katada. Goro had been hired by an American game company called TIP-G, something he had dreamed of for a long time, and he had gone to America. Fumiko had gone back knowing full well that she could not change the present. And while in the past, Goro had told her that he wanted her to wait three years.

His words were a hint, suggesting after three years they should get married. But upon returning from America three years later, he was immediately sent to work in Germany. Yet they remained engaged and finally, last year, after various obstacles, the path was clear for them to get married. So Fumiko became Mrs Katada.

In response to Kurata's reaction, Nagare pulled a long face

and looked conflicted. The coffee was not going to stay warm for ever.

'You were just saying that it wasn't Fumiko that you were waiting for, is that right?' Nagare asked, recalling how the conversation had gone sideways because Miki had mistaken Fumiko's surname.

'That's right, not Fumiko.'

'Then who are you waiting for?'

'She, um, she's a work colleague. Her name is Asami Mori,' Kurata replied, sounding a little flustered. 'I asked Ms Kiyokawa, I mean Fumiko, to bring her here.' He looked over to the entrance, despite no one having come in.

The person Kurata had come to see was Asami Mori, a junior work colleague of Fumiko's. Kurata and Asami had joined at the same time, but Kurata had been in Sales while Asami was assigned to the Development department, where Fumiko worked.

Nagare had no idea why Kurata had come from the past to meet his colleague, and he had no intention of asking.

'Oh . . . I see. Well, I hope they arrive soon,' Nagare muttered, and Kurata smiled a little.

'If they don't come, they don't come. I'm fine with that,' he replied.

'What do you mean?' Nagare asked.

'We got engaged, but it doesn't look like we will get married now . . .' he said, looking down glumly.

*Has he come to meet his ex-fiancée out of concern?*

Kurata's deflated expression was enough to give Nagare a general idea of the circumstances.

'Oh, I see,' he said and refrained from commenting further.

'But finding out that Ms Kiyokawa got married made it worthwhile coming. I am so, so glad about that.'

Kurata smiled happily. He was not faking it. He looked genuinely pleased. Miki, who was sitting opposite Kurata resting her cheek on her hand, had been listening to the exchange.

'Why did Fumiko change her name?' she asked Nagare.

'You change your name when you get married,' Nagare said, sounding a little irritated, like a parent who is bombarded with similar questions every day.

'What? Me as well? When I get married, will I change my name too?'

'If you get married.'

'Huh? No way. Hey, Mistress, will you change your name?' She looked at Kazu.

Recently, Miki had started calling Kazu 'Mistress'. No one exactly knew why. Several days earlier, it had been 'Sister Kazu'; before that, 'Sister', and before that, simply 'Kazu'. It was as if Kazu's rank had been slowly and steadily rising.

'Mistress, are you going to change your name if you get married?'

'If I get married.' Responding to Miki in her usual cool way, she carried on wiping glasses.

'Oh . . . I see,' Miki replied.

It was unclear what Miki 'saw', but she nodded and returned to the seat at the counter to start writing some more wishes for the *tanzaku*.

*Beep-boop beep-boop . . . Beep-boop beep-boop . . .*

The phone began ringing from the back room. Kazu was about to go and answer it, but Nagare put his hand up to stop her and disappeared into the back room himself.

*Beep-boop . . .*

Kurata dropped his eyes to the tabletop and stared at what he had written on his *tanzaku*.

Despite being two years his junior, Asami Mori never spoke to him in the kind of polite language normally used with more senior employees, because they joined the company at the same time. As a person full of smiles who appeared to be completely genuine, she was popular, including within the company.

Fumiko, who worked in the same office as Asami, was popular for her looks, but at work she was called a bitch behind her back. That made Asami's presence there all the more welcome as she helped soften the war-room atmosphere that would hang in the office when a deadline approached.

Kurata and Asami would often go out drinking with people who had joined at the same time. Conversations would often centre around work grievances, but Kurata never once bad-mouthed the company or his superiors. On the contrary, he always looked on the bright side, and he showed leadership when the going got tough and the situation hopeless.

Asami saw Kurata as an extremely positive guy, but she had a boyfriend when she joined the company and never really thought of him as a 'man'.

Kurata and Asami grew close, however, when Asami

discussed her miscarriage with him. She had miscarried a child just after she had broken up with her boyfriend. She hadn't known that she was pregnant until after the split, and the miscarriage was unrelated to the shock of breaking up. Asami had a condition which meant she was more likely to suffer a miscarriage.

When she found out that she was pregnant, she had decided to keep the baby, even if it meant being a single mum. Having made this choice, the news that she was more prone to miscarriage came as an even bigger shock. She couldn't help but feel that it was her fault.

Overwhelmed by guilt, she shared her feelings with her close friends outside work, her parents, and her sister. Although they tried to console and comfort her in her time of sadness, none of them could offer words that dispelled the clouds from her heart.

It was while she was in this state that Kurata came up to her and asked, 'Is something wrong?'

She didn't think that he would understand the delicate subject of losing a baby, being a man and all. But she desperately needed a sympathetic ear – it did not matter whose it was. Of the people she had already told, her female friends had cried with her, and her parents had tried to reassure her by telling her it wasn't her fault. She therefore assumed that Kurata, likewise, would empathize and tell her something to console her. So, she spoke honestly of her feelings.

However, after he listened to her story, his first response was to ask how many days she had carried the baby. After she told him ten weeks, or about seventy days, he asked, 'Why do you think the child you were carrying was granted life in this world for those seventy days?'

This sparked so much anger in Asami, her lips began to tremble.

'Are you really asking why it was given life?' Her eyes flushed red, she sobbed convulsively. 'Are you telling me I'm a bad person?'

She found herself unable to stop herself from snapping at him like this. She had already blamed herself for her child never having been born. But to then be told this by someone who had absolutely no businesses in saying such a thing made her even more distraught.

Kurata seemed to understand what she meant and smiled kindly. 'No, you've got it wrong.'

'What have I got wrong? The child I was carrying could do nothing! I couldn't even let it be born! It was my fault! I was only able to give that child seventy days of life! Only seventy days!'

With a composed expression, he calmly waited for her to stop crying, and then said, 'That child used its seventy-day-long life for your happiness.'

He spoke gently, but with unwavering certainty.

'If you remain devastated like this, then your child will have used those seventy days in vain.'

His message was not one of empathy. He was pointing out a way Asami could change the way she thought about the grief that she was experiencing.

'But if you try to find happiness after this, then this child will have put those seventy days towards making you happy. In that case, its life has meaning. You are the one who is able to create meaning for why that child was granted life. There-fore, you absolutely must try to be happy. The one person who would want that for you the most is that child.'

On hearing these words, Asami gasped. The deep des-pair that had been weighing on her heart began to shift, and everything before her appeared a little brighter.

*By trying to be happy, I can give meaning to this child's life.*

That was the clear answer.

She was unable to hold back tears. She looked up to the heavens and wailed loudly as she sobbed. Her tears were less from sadness than from joy at seeing a way out from the bottomless pit and experiencing something like happiness again.

That was the moment that Kurata became more than just a very positive guy.

'Mr Kurata?'

Kurata suddenly noticed that Nagare was standing next to him with the phone in his hand.

'Huh, yes?'

'It's Fumiko.'

'Oh . . . thank you.'

He took the handset. 'Yes, it's Kurata here.'

Kurata had said if he didn't meet her, he would be fine with that. Nevertheless, his expression hardened a little, as if he was nervous to speak to her on the phone.

'Uh-huh, yes . . . Oh, really? . . . I see . . . No, not at all . . . Thank you so much.'

Based only on witnessing his side of the call, he didn't seem particularly let down. As he spoke, he sat up with his chest puffed out awkwardly and looked straight ahead, as if Fumiko was sitting there in front of him. Nagare stood observing his unnaturally tense pose with a look of concern.

'No, no. You have done so much for me . . . That's quite OK . . . thank you very much.'

He bowed his head very deeply.

'Right . . . yes . . . OK, uh-huh . . . the coffee will be cold soon, so . . . yes . . .'

He glanced at the clock on the wall in the middle.

Of the three antique clocks on the wall, only the one in the centre showed the right time. Of the other two, one was fast and one was slow. Accordingly, when Nagare, Kazu or any of the regulars wanted to check the time, they would always look at the one in the middle.

Judging by Kurata's conversation on the phone with Fumiko, Nagare was assuming that the woman he was waiting for, Asami, was not coming.

'Yes, yes . . .'

He reached out and touched the cup to check the temperature of the coffee.

*I've hardly any time left . . .*

Kurata took a very deep breath and slowly closed his eyes. Kazu watched him do this, but did nothing.

'Oh, that reminds me. I heard you got married. Congratulations. Yes, the cafe staff told me . . . believe me, hearing that alone made my trip worth it.'

They weren't just empty words, he really seemed to mean

it. His beaming face was seemingly directed to Fumiko, wherever she was.

'. . . Bye.'

Kurata slowly ended the call. Nagare quietly approached the table, and Kurata returned the handset to him.

'I'll go back now,' he said softly.

He was smiling but his voice was faltering. He clearly seemed disappointed that he had come all this way to the future only to miss out on meeting Asami.

'Anything we can do before you go?' Nagare said, observing Kurata.

Nagare knew he couldn't offer anything. But he couldn't help asking. He kept pressing the buttons on the handset pointlessly.

Kurata must have noticed how he was feeling.

'No, everything is fine. Thank you very much,' he replied with a smile.

Nagare slowly lifted his head and walked off towards the back room holding on to the handset.

'Could you put this up for me, please?' Kurata asked, presenting the *tanzaku* bearing his wish.

'Yes, sir,' said Miki. Because Kurata couldn't leave his chair, she came and took it from him.

'Thank you for everything,' he said, and bowing his head to Kazu behind the counter, he picked up the cup in front of him.

In the summer, two and a half years ago . . .

Kurata had been diagnosed with acute myelogenous leu-kaemia. He was told he could start treatment and hope to survive, or forgo it and be left with only six months to live. It was the second summer of his relationship with Asami. He'd got the news of his diagnosis just after deciding to get a ring ready secretly and propose to her.

But he didn't give up. If it meant the slightest chance of survival, he had no trouble deciding to begin treatment. It was then he decided to carry out his plan, keeping it a secret from Asami. He had heard from Fumiko that in this cafe, not only could you return to the past, but you could also travel to the future. The information he obtained from Fumiko, however, wasn't detailed enough for him to carry out his plan successfully. So he visited the cafe to find out first-hand whether the plan he had conceived could work.

Getting there was no trouble as he had visited it on two prior occasions when he had tagged along with Fumiko. But just as the weather forecast had predicted, he got caught in sporadic torrential downpours. Even using an umbrella, he was still soaked from the waist down by the time he entered the cafe.

Maybe because of the rain, only the waitress, Kazu, and the woman in the dress were in the cafe. Kurata quickly intro-duced himself and began explaining his plan to Kazu.

'I wish to go to the future. Ms Kiyokawa told me that you could also go to the future when you sit on that chair,' he said, looking at the woman in the dress. He pulled out a notebook on which he had jotted down as much detail on the rules as possible, based on what Fumiko had told him, and then began to check if they were right or not.

'When returning to the past, you cannot meet anyone who has not visited the cafe. What about the future? Is it impossible to meet the person you want to meet unless they come to the cafe?'

'That's right,' replied Kazu matter-of-factly while carrying on with her work. Proceeding methodically with his questions while referring to his notebook, Kurata confirmed that the woman in the dress left her seat to go to the toilet once a day and that even when travelling to the future, it was not possible to stand up from the chair.

'Is the time it takes for the coffee to get cold the same for everyone? Or does the time become longer or shorter depending on the circumstances?' he asked.

This was a shrewd question. If the time it took for the coffee to get cold was consistently the same, he could check with Fumiko, who had gone back in time, and get a good idea of how long he would have. But if the duration was different each time, in the worst-case scenario, he could get less time than her.

When going to the past, you know exactly when the person you want to meet visited the cafe. That means you can aim for a specific time and go back with pinpoint precision. So even if the time allowed there was short, you'd most likely meet them.

The same doesn't apply to the future. You can arrange to meet someone, but whether they arrive at that time depends on circumstances you cannot predict. You might end up missing them by only a few seconds.

Any difference in the amount of time you had was therefore quite an important point. Kurata swallowed while waiting for Kazu's answer.

'I don't know,' she replied bluntly.

Kurata didn't seem overly disappointed, though, as if he had expected such an answer.

'Oh, OK,' he replied simply. Then he asked his last question.

'When you go to the past, there is nothing you can do that will change the present. Would it be right to think that this applies to when you visit the future as well?'

Unlike the previous questions, on this question, Kazu stopped what she was doing and thought for a moment.

'I think so,' she replied. Maybe it was because she had some idea why Kurata was asking this question, but it was rare for her to provide such a vague answer. That said, it was the first time anyone had ever asked this question.

Kurata thought that if the rule 'no matter what you do while in the past, the present won't change' applied for going to the future too . . .

. . . if he went to the future and didn't meet her, then no matter what he did from then on, that future would not change. Or on the other hand, if he did meet her in the future, then no matter what he did from then on, that meeting would still take place.

Of all the rules, this was the rule he had really wanted to clarify.

To simply go to the future and put his trust in meeting by chance was ill-advised. If Asami was a cafe regular, then that might be possible. But she wasn't. Kurata intended to plan meticulously to get her to visit the cafe at the same time as him in the future.

If the future could be changed, then first he would go from now to the future, and even if he did not meet Asami that time, upon returning, he would just need to work harder so they would meet next time.

But that was not the case.

The future reality of the time you travelled to could not be changed.

This was not a new rule. It was just an extension of the rule that no matter how hard you tried while in the past, you couldn't change the present. Kurata, who was intending to travel to the future, was the only person ever to have considered it.

He seemed to mull it over for a little while.

'Hmmm. I see. Thank you very much,' he said bowing his head.

'Are you wishing to travel today?' she asked.

'No, not today,' he replied. And squeaking and squelching in his still-wet shoes, he left the cafe.

In order to meet Asami in the future, Kurata decided to recruit Fumiko as his co-conspirator. Fumiko frequently visited the cafe, and she was good friends with Asami. He was also impressed with her excellent work as a systems engineer, and was convinced that there was no one better suited to the task.

Kurata called Fumiko, telling her he wanted to meet to discuss something. Then he got straight to the point.

'I probably only have about six months to live,' he said. Showing a shocked Fumiko his test results, he explained what his doctor had told him and that he would be going into hospital in a week's time. Naturally, Fumiko was lost for words, but the seriousness of his face left her no choice but to accept the news.

'What do you want me to do?' she asked.

First he told her, 'It is something that I can trust only you to do.' Then he announced, 'I am going to go to that cafe and travel to two and a half years in the future. If I'm dead, could you bring Asami to the cafe?'

Fumiko gave Kurata a complicated look upon hearing him say, *If I'm dead*.

'However, under either of the following two conditions, you don't need to ask her to come.'

'What do you mean by I don't need to ask her to come?'

Fumiko's expression showed she was clearly struggling with what he was saying. He asked her to bring Asami to the cafe in two and a half years, then he gave her conditions for when she didn't have to bring her. She couldn't understand what he had in mind at all.

But, unperturbed, he proceeded to outline the conditions.

'First, if I don't die, then you don't need to bring her.'

This made sense. After all, that was the most desirable situation. But when she heard the second condition, Fumiko was lost for words.

'If, after I die, Asami is married and is living a happy life, then please don't bring her.'

'What? That makes no sense to me at all . . .'

'If I don't meet Asami when I travel to the future, then I will take that to mean she is happily married, and I will return. But if that is not the case, then there is something that I want to say to her . . . that's why . . .'

Kurata may have been told he had only six months to live, but the one thing he wanted was for Asami to be happy.

On hearing his plan, Fumiko said, 'People like you . . .' and began to cry.

Everything depended on her deciding whether to ask Asami or not.

'Ideally, you will never need to do anything, but please, do what you can,' he said, bowing his head deeply.

But Asami hadn't turned up. He let out a short breath and brought the cup he held to his lips. Just then . . .

CLANG-DONG

The doorbell rang and soon after, rushing into the cafe, was Asami Mori, wearing a navy-blue duffel coat.

It must have started snowing outside, as there was a scattering of snowflakes on her head and shoulders. Kurata was in short sleeves, having come from summer in the past. When Asami suddenly showed up in a coat bearing the signs of a white Christmas, it wasn't clear what season their meeting was taking place in. The two regarded each other for a moment in silence.

'Hi there!' Kurata said awkwardly.

Asami was still catching her breath, but she was staring at him rather crossly.

'Fumiko told me everything. What were you thinking? Making me come and meet a dead person, did you put yourself in my shoes for even a second?' she said brusquely. Staring into Asami's face, Kurata began awkwardly needling his forehead with his index finger.

'Sorry,' he muttered. He continued to stare, as if observing her closely.

'What?' Asami asked suspiciously.

'. . . Oh sorry, nothing. I have to go back,' he said softly, as if he had messed up. As he was bringing the cup to his lips, Asami approached him. She held out her left hand for him to see. On her third finger was a sparkling ring.

'Look, I am married, OK?' she declared, staring straight into his eyes, pronouncing her words clearly and tersely.

'Uh-huh.' Kurata's eyes were getting red. Asami looked away from him, and sighed.

'It's been two years since you died. What were you thinking, getting Fumiko entangled like that? Did you ever consider that you were worrying too much?' she said accusingly.

'It certainly seems I didn't need to be so worried . . .' Kurata said happily with a bitter-sweet smile. It was unclear what Asami was thinking, showing up like that, but hearing that she was married was all the satisfaction he needed.

'I have to go.'

After returning to the past, he would have six months left to live. By coming to the future, he hadn't changed the fact that he would die. But that knowledge had not darkened his expression one little bit. His smiling face was bright, full of cheer and happiness.

Asami, unable to read his thoughts, simply faced him with her arms crossed.

'Right then . . .'

He drank all the coffee in one go. Immediately, he began to feel dizzy. His surroundings began to shimmer. As he returned the cup to the saucer, his hands began gradually to turn into vapour. As his body floated in space, Asami spoke.

'Kurata!' she yelled.

His consciousness was beginning to cloud and his surroundings were beginning to flow past him.

'Thanks for co—'

His hearing was cut off abruptly, and he disappeared as if he had been sucked up into the ceiling.

Suddenly the woman in the dress appeared in the chair that he had been sitting in, like a mirage. Asami just stood there, staring at the space where he had vanished.

CLANG-DONG

The sharp sound of the doorbell rang out.

Fumiko came in, dressed for winter in a down jacket and wool-lined boots. She had been standing there with the door half open, listening to the conversation between the two former lovers, waiting for it to end.

She walked slowly up to Asami.

'Asami . . .' she said.

There were two conditions under which Kurata had asked Fumiko not to bring Asami.

One, if he had not died; and –

Two, if he had died, but Asami was married and happy.

But after he had died, Fumiko had worried about when best to tell Asami, right up until the day before the meeting would take place.

When it came to the condition that she *didn't have to bring Asami if she was married and happy*, she interpreted that to mean, *if Asami can't get over Kurata and is unable to marry anyone else, then he wants her to come.*

If Asami was doing her best to forget Kurata and put him behind her, however, Fumiko didn't want to make her meet him just because she wasn't married.

It would be a meeting with someone who was dead: not something to be taken lightly. Badly handled, it could really mess up Asami's life. Fumiko mulled over the different possibilities incessantly, but two years went by with no solution to her worries nor any insight into Asami's feelings.

Asami mourned Kurata after his death, but after about six months, she went on with her life. From what Fumiko could see, Asami had not let his death hold her back.

But based on this alone, Fumiko was unable to decide whether to bring Asami along on the day set for the meeting. Asami hadn't married, but whether someone was married or not was no measure of their happiness. But Fumiko had not heard anything close to a romantic rumour about Asami since Kurata died. Then, before she knew it, the chosen day was only a week away.

After much agonizing, Fumiko decided to consult her

husband, Goro. Although she recognized his prowess as a fellow systems engineer, her faith in him normally didn't extend to affairs of the heart. However, they had agreed that if either of them had any troubles, they would talk it over as a couple. So, clutching at straws, she sought his advice.

When she did, Goro looked at her with a serious expression.

'I don't think he considered that you would worry so much over it,' he pronounced.

Fumiko didn't know what he was talking about.

'He had complete faith in you.'

'But I don't know what I should do!'

'No, no. He didn't have faith in you as a woman.'

'Huh? What are you saying?'

'He had faith in you as a systems engineer.'

'What do you mean?'

'Think about what he said. The conditions for which he didn't want you to bring Asami were, one, if he had not died, and two, if after he died she was married and happy.'

'OK.'

'If you see it simply as a program that judges whether those conditions apply, you can dismiss any other conditions as not in the program . . .'

'If Kurata's conditions don't apply, you go ahead.'

'Right. For example, she might be happy, but she is not married. That doesn't meet his conditions for not bringing her.'

'. . . I see.'

'Probably, knowing Asami better than you, Kurata set

those absolute conditions as part of a way to help her recover from some kind of trauma.'

Now that he mentioned it, Fumiko had an idea what that trauma might be. Asami had had a miscarriage. She had also heard Asami say, *It's so scary to think I might have another.*

'In contrast, there is also the case where she is married but not happy, isn't there? That case doesn't meet the conditions of not bringing her either.'

'OK. I get it now. Thank you!' she said and immediately set off to meet Asami.

Fumiko always acted swiftly once she knew what needed doing. The agreed day and time of the meeting in the cafe was 7 p.m. on 25 December, Christmas Day. She of course didn't reveal Kurata's conditions when she told Asami that he was coming from the past at that time, but on hearing the news, Asami's voice seemed to fade.

'I see . . .' she acknowledged, her mood visibly darkening.

When the day of Kurata's visit arrived, Asami was absent from work without notice. People had tried contacting her, but she didn't answer. Her colleagues started half-jokingly suggesting that she must have thought Christmas was more important than work. Only Fumiko knew the circumstances for her absence. 'Less talk and more work, if you please,' she ordered her team in a brisk manner.

Asami was probably agonizing over whether to meet him. Fumiko sent her a text.

*I'll be waiting in front of the cafe tonight at 7 p.m.*

*

That night . . .

Around the station there stood many Christmas trees, decorated with lights that shone and sparkled. The place was bustling with people, and Christmas songs played from all directions. The cafe, however, was located on a side street, nestled among buildings some ten minutes' walk from the station. Apart from a small wreath attached to the cafe's sign, it was the same as any other day. The only light came from the main street, making it very dark. Compared to the liveliness of the area around the station, it felt lonely.

Fumiko stood waiting outside the ground-floor entrance.

'Has it always been this dark?' she muttered to herself, watching her foggy white breath.

Snow, which had been coming down in sprinkles since sunset, danced and fluttered, even in this narrow side street. Even an umbrella held to the sky collected only a tiny amount of snow.

She pulled her sleeve back from her glove, far enough to check her watch. It was already a little later than when she had agreed to meet Kurata.

But Asami had not shown up.

Her train might have been delayed because of the snow, which was also causing congestion on the roads as it settled. Normally, she would have rejoiced at such a romantic white Christmas. But tonight, this snow was a nuisance, causing her brow to furrow.

'Asami . . . where are you?'

Fumiko tried phoning her a third time, but there was still no answer.

*They're not going to meet. She's probably decided not to come.*

She felt a little despondent at Asami's decision, but it was her choice to make.

*I should have used a bit more coercion to get her to come.*

She was feeling a little apologetic and a little put-out.

*What can I say to Kurata?*

She was right outside the cafe, but she couldn't face going in. She decided to talk to Kurata on the phone instead.

'Er, Kurata, is that you? It's Fumiko Kiyokawa . . . Uh-huh . . . About Asami . . . It's all a little complicated . . . I told her that you're coming today . . . I only told her a week ago . . . Right . . . Yeah, I'm so sorry. I overthought it . . . Anyway, it sounded like she was coming. Yeah . . . Uh-huh . . . Hu-hum, but she's well. She was really sad for about six months, I guess. But she seems over it now . . . Yes . . . I'm really sorry. I'm thinking now I should have tried harder. I'm regretting it now . . . Huh? . . . Oh, yes. Thank you . . . Oh, you have to go soon? Goodness me . . . Anyway, I'm truly sorry . . . Yes, OK then . . .'

After she ended the call, she couldn't help a nagging feeling of regret. The snow was cold and falling a little heavier now.

*I may as well go home.*

She had dragged her heavy foot one step, when . . .

'Fumiko!' said a woman's voice behind her. Fumiko turned around to see a very out-of-breath Asami standing there.

'Asami!'

'Fumiko, is Kurata . . . still here?'

'I'm not sure, but . . .'

She looked at her watch. He had said he would come at

seven and it was now eight minutes past. Even if by good luck his coffee had not gone cold, he might have drunk it after ending the phone call. There wasn't a second to lose.

'Let's go!' urged Fumiko as she put her hand on Asami's back and guided her down the stairs.

In front of the cafe door, Asami turned to her.

'I need to borrow your wedding ring,' she requested.

The ring was very special to Fumiko, and she had only received it last year.

*I'll ask later.*

Not hesitating, she quickly pulled the ring from her finger and presented it to Asami.

'OK, hurry!'

'Thank you!' Asami nodded her head in thanks and entered the cafe as the doorbell rang.

Staring at the space where Kurata had vanished, Asami let out a soft sigh.

'I tried to move on, but I couldn't forget Kurata . . . I ended up thinking I could never marry anyone else but him,' she said, as her body shook slightly.

Looking at Asami, Fumiko just said, 'Uh-huh.' She could imagine being in her shoes.

*I would feel the same if it were me.*

She clenched her hand on her chest, she couldn't find the words to say anything else.

'But I remembered what he told me when I had my miscarriage. He told me that little baby had used the seventy days of its life to bring happiness into my life. He said that if I couldn't find a way out of my unhappiness, then that would have been the result of the baby's seventy days. But if I could find a way to be happy again, that is what the baby's life would have brought me. Through that choice, I could allow its life to have meaning. I could create a reason for why my child was granted life. He told me that was why I had to try to be happy. He said that no one would have wished that more than my child.'

She stopped and started, relaying what Kurata had told her in a soft and trembling voice.

'So, it made me think. I might not be able to get married right now, but I absolutely must be happy.'

'Asami . . .'

'Because if my happiness could become his happiness . . .'

Asami pulled the borrowed ring from her finger and gave it back to Fumiko. To make Kurata believe that she had got married, she had borrowed Fumiko's ring and lied.

'I wish that Asami is happy always,' read Miki aloud from the *tanzaku* that Kurata had left.

Asami didn't know how that *tanzaku* existed. But as soon as she heard it, she knew they were Kurata's words. Large tears began to flow down her cheeks all at once, and she collapsed in a heap on the floor.

'Are you all right, miss?' Miki asked, peering down at Asami in puzzlement.

Fumiko put her arm around Asami's shoulder, and Kazu stopped working and looked over at the woman in the dress.

*

That day, Nagare closed the cafe early.

When she returned home, Fumiko told Goro what had happened.

'I think it's likely that Kurata knew she was lying,' he said after she had finished, taking the cake he had bought out of its box.

'You think he knew? Why?' Fumiko asked, frowning a little.

'She told him that you had told her everything, right?'

'Yes, she did, but what of it?'

'If she had really been happily married, why would there be any need for you to explain it all to her? Based on his conditions, in that scenario, you didn't have to bring her.'

'Oh . . .'

'Do you see?'

'Oh no, I hadn't thought of that. I told her everything . . . It's my fault . . .'

Looking at Fumiko's face becoming more and more disappointed, Goro suddenly chuckled.

'What? What are you laughing at?' she demanded as her expression shifted to indignation.

Goro quickly apologized, saying sorry several times. After which, he said, 'I don't think it matters. Even if he knew she lied, he returned to the past without saying anything because he knew she would now find happiness and perhaps get married . . .'

On saying this, Goro held out a Christmas present he had got her, to take her mind off the subject.

'You've had the same experience, haven't you?'

'I have?'

'In terms of her unhappiness here in the present, when she came to the cafe, there was nothing he could have done to change that . . .'

'But what about the future?'

'Exactly! He knew that her lie had altered how she really felt.'

'You mean she decided right then to be happy?'

'Yes. That's why he returned to the past without saying anything.'

'. . . I see.'

'So, you can put your mind at ease,' Goro said, spearing a piece of cake with his fork.

'. . . Well, that's all right, then,' she said, looking relieved as she followed his lead and took a mouthful of cake.

Time passed ever so silently that Christmas night.

After the cafe was closed . . .

The lamps were turned off and only the Christmas lights illuminated the room. Kazu, who had closed the cash register and changed into her own clothes, was standing in front of the woman in the dress. She was simply standing there idly, without a reason.

**CLANG-DONG**

'You're still here,' observed Nagare with Miki on his back, she had tired herself out and fallen asleep from playing in the snow.

'. . . Yeah.'

'Were you thinking about Kurata?'

Rather than answering, Kazu just looked at Miki sleeping peacefully on Nagare's back.

He didn't ask any more questions. He simply walked by Kazu, and just before leaving the room . . .

'Kaname feels the same, I think,' he said softly, as if talking to himself, and then disappeared into the back room.

As the only source of illumination, the lights adorning the ceiling-tall Christmas tree shone vividly on Kazu's back as she lingered in the quiet cafe.

On the day that Kaname had gone to meet her dead husband, it had been seven-year-old Kazu who had served her the coffee. When Nagare, who had been present in the cafe on that fateful day, had been asked what happened by an acquaintance who knew Kaname, he had quietly said the following.

'When she heard mention of the coffee being cold, she probably imagined that temperature to be cold like tap water. But there are other people who think a coffee is cold when it is below skin temperature. So, when it comes to that rule, no one really knows what "when the coffee gets cold" means. Kaname probably just thought the coffee hadn't gone cold yet.'

However, no one knows the truth of the matter. Everyone had told the young Kazu, 'Kazu, you're not to blame.'

But in her heart, she felt . . .

*I'm the one who poured Mum the coffee . . .*
She could never erase that fact.
As the days passed, she began to feel . . .
*I'm the one who killed Mum . . .*

The experience took away Kazu's innocence and robbed her of her smile. She began roaming around aimlessly like a sleepwalker both day and night. Losing the ability to concentrate, she walked in the middle of the road and nearly got hit by a car. Once she was discovered in a river in the middle of winter. However, she never had a conscious death wish. It was subconscious. Kazu continually blamed herself in her subconscious.

One day, three years after the event, she was standing at a railway crossing. Her expression was not of a girl who wished to die. She gazed at the bleating alert system with a cool, unreadable expression as it rang out.

The sinking evening sun gave the town an orange hue. Behind Kazu, also waiting for the crossing gate to open, were a mother and her child coming back from shopping and a group of students on their way home. From the crowd came a voice.

'Mummy, I'm sorry,' said a child. It was just a casual good-natured conversation between mother and child.

Kazu stood for a moment looking at the two of them.

Then mumbling, 'Mum . . .' she started walking towards the crossing gate as if it was pulling her towards it.

Just then . . .

'Do you mind taking me with you?'

The speaker of those words had quietly come up beside

her. She was Kinuyo, the teacher at the neighbourhood art school. By chance she had also been at the cafe on the day Kaname returned to the past. It had pained her to see Kazu's smiling face disappear after that fateful day, and she had constantly been at Kazu's side, watching out for her.

But up until that day, no matter what she tried saying to her, she couldn't seem to rescue her heart. When she said, 'Take me with you,' she meant that she wanted to stick by this girl who suffered and was so anguished.

The young Kazu was suffering because she felt that her mother's death was her fault. Kinuyo thought that if Kazu couldn't escape from these feelings, they would both go to the place where Kaname was, so that they could bow their heads together.

But Kazu's reaction to those words was unlike anything she expected. Tears flowed from her eyes for the first time since Kaname's death and she wailed loudly. Kinuyo didn't know what had permeated Kazu's heart. She only knew that she had been suffering alone up until then, and that she didn't want to die.

Standing there together next to the tracks as the trains roared and whooshed past for what seemed like for ever, Kinuyo hugged Kazu tightly and stroked her head until she stopped crying.

As time passed, the two were swallowed up by the evening darkness.

After that day, Kazu once again began pouring the coffee for customers who said they wanted to return to the past.

*

*Dong . . . Dong . . .*

The clock in the centre on the wall in the cafe chimed to announce it was two o'clock in the morning.

In the middle of the night, everything was silent. As the ceiling fan rotated slowly, Kaname was as usual quietly reading the novel that Kazu had provided.

Resembling a still-life object that had been blended into a painting of the cafe, Kazu was completely motionless – except for a single teardrop, running down her cheek.

# IV

*The Married Couple*

---

People tend to feel happy when spring arrives, especially after a cold winter.

When spring begins, however, cannot be pinpointed to one particular moment. There is no one day that clearly marks when winter ends and spring begins. Spring hides inside winter. We notice it emerging with our eyes, our skin and other senses. We find it in new buds, a comfortable breeze and the warmth of the sun. It exists alongside winter.

'Is your mind still on Kaname?' asked Nagare Tokita, as if speaking to himself. He was sitting on a counter stool dexterously folding paper napkins into cranes.

Nagare's muttering was directed at Kazu Tokita, who was behind him. But Kazu continued to wipe the table silently and adjusted the position of the coaster on which the sugar pot sat.

Nagare placed the seventh paper crane on the table.

'I think you should have the baby,' he said, directing his thin almond-shaped eyes at Kazu as she went about her work. 'I think Kaname definitely—'

CLANG-DONG

The sound of the doorbell cut him off mid-sentence, but neither Nagare nor Kazu said, 'Hello, welcome.'

In this cafe, once a visitor had come through the door with the bell attached to it, they had to cross the hall before entering the room. Nagare watched the entrance in silence.

After a moment, Kiyoshi Manda appeared looking sheepish. Kiyoshi was a detective who had reached retirement age that spring. He wore a trench coat and an old hunting cap, and looked like a detective in a TV police drama from the seventies. Despite being a detective, there was nothing intimidating or hard about him. He was about the same height as Kazu and smiled often. He resembled any other sociable man in his later years, whom you might meet anywhere.

The hands of the clock in the middle of the wall were pointing to ten minutes to eight. The cafe closed at eight.

'Is it all right?' he asked tentatively.

Kazu replied as always, 'Yes, come in,' but Nagare just nodded in a somewhat subdued manner.

When Kiyoshi visited the cafe, he would always sit at the table closest to the entrance and order a coffee. But today, instead of sitting in his regular chair, he stood in the same place, uncertainly.

'Please, take a seat,' offered Kazu from behind the counter

as she presented him with a glass of water and gestured for him to sit down.

Kiyoshi raised his tattered hunting cap politely. 'Thank you,' he replied and sat on a stool, leaving the one between him and Nagare vacant.

Nagare carefully gathered together the paper cranes and asked, 'Will it be a coffee as usual?' as he stood up and started heading for the kitchen.

'Er, no, actually. Today . . .' and as Nagare paused on his way to the kitchen, Kiyoshi looked over at the woman in the dress. Nagare followed Kiyoshi's gaze and narrowed his eyes.

'Oh?'

'Actually, I've come to give this . . .' he said, pulling out a small box, the kind a pen might come in, wrapped up like a present, '. . . to my wife.'

'Is that . . . ?' asked Kazu, recognizing it.

'Yes. It's the necklace you helped choose for me,' replied Kiyoshi bashfully as he scratched his head through his hunting cap.

The previous autumn Kiyoshi had asked for advice on what would make a good birthday present for his wife. Kazu had suggested a necklace. In the end, unable to decide by himself, Kiyoshi took her along with him to help him choose it.

'I had promised to give it to her here, but when the day came, I was called in for an emergency and I never did . . .'

Listening to Kiyoshi's words, Nagare locked eyes with Kazu. 'So, are you saying you want to return to your wife's birthday?' he asked.

'Yes.'

Nagare bit his lip and went silent. Two or three seconds passed with no one saying a word. Sitting in the quiet cafe, it must have seemed a very long stretch of silence to Kiyoshi.

'Don't worry, it's all right. I know the rules well,' he hastened to add.

Even with that, however, Nagare maintained his silence as the crevices in his brow deepened.

Kiyoshi could tell there was something strange about his reaction.

'What is it?' he asked uneasily.

'I don't mean to be rude, but I don't see why you have to return to the past just to give your wife a present,' he said, in a soft apologetic voice.

Kiyoshi nodded, as if he now understood the reason for Nagare's awkward silence. 'Ha, ha, ha. For sure . . . I see what you are saying . . .' he said, scratching his head.

'I'm sorry.' Nagare bowed his head hastily.

'No, no. It's fine . . . It's my fault for not providing a proper explanation,' Kiyoshi said, reaching out to pick up the glass that Kazu had served him. He took a small sip.

'Explanation?'

'Yes,' Kiyoshi replied. 'It was exactly one year ago when I found out that you can return to the past in this cafe.'

Kiyoshi's *explanation* was going right back to when he first visited this cafe.

CLANG-DONG

When Kiyoshi walked in, a red-faced man was crying at the far table, and a frail elderly woman was sitting opposite him. At the counter was a boy about elementary-school age and behind the counter was a man two metres tall, presumably a staff member.

The tall man did not greet Kiyoshi as he entered the cafe. He was too busy watching the couple at the far table. Only the young boy, who was slurping his orange juice through a straw, was staring at Kiyoshi.

*Not being noticed when entering a cafe is nothing to make a fuss about. I'm sure he'll notice me in a moment . . .* Kiyoshi nodded to the boy in acknowledgement and took a seat at the table closest to the entrance.

As soon as he had sat down, the crying man was suddenly enveloped in a puff of vapour. And then he seemed to vanish, sucked up into the ceiling.

*What?*

As Kiyoshi stared with bulging eyes, a woman wearing a white dress appeared in the chair that the man had vanished from. These bizarre events seemed like something you might see in a magic show.

*What happened just now?*

As he watched in amazement, the elderly woman was talking to the woman in the white dress. From what he could pick up, she was saying, 'Now, if there was only something I could do to make Kazu happy . . .'

The old woman was Kinuyo Mita and the man who had disappeared was Kinuyo's son, Yukio. It was upon witnessing this incident that Kiyoshi came to realize that you really could return to the past in this cafe.

When he later learned from Kazu and Nagare about the annoying rules that applied when travelling back in time, he was astonished that anyone would want to make the journey. *If it is not possible to change the present no matter how hard you try while in the past, then why bother?* He became very interested in learning about the people who, even after knowing the rules, decided to go back.

'. . . It was rude of me, I know, but I decided to look into the people who have returned to the past here.'

Kiyoshi bowed his head at Nagare, still paused in the entrance to the kitchen, and Kazu, who was standing behind the counter.

'I found out from my investigation . . .' Kiyoshi brought out a small black notebook before continuing, '. . . that over the last thirty years, forty-one people have sat in that chair and travelled back in time. They each had their own reasons for doing so, to meet a lover, a husband, a daughter, and so forth, but of those forty-one people, four returned to the past to meet someone who had died.

'There were two last year, one seven years ago, and then there was your mother twenty-two years ago . . . four people.'

Listening to Kiyoshi's explanation, Nagare's face seemed to turn blue.

'How on earth did you learn all that?' he asked. In contrast with Nagare's troubled expression, Kazu was staring into space vacantly.

Kiyoshi inhaled slowly.

'Kinuyo told me all this before she died,' he said sympathetically, and looked at Kazu.

On hearing his words, she lowered her gaze.

'The last thing she told me was that she thought of you as her daughter,' he said.

Kazu closed her eyes slowly.

'I was very curious. I wondered why there were four people who, despite knowing the rule that you cannot change the present no matter how hard you try, were able to go and meet people who had died.' Kiyoshi turned the page of his notebook.

'There was one woman who went back to meet her younger sister, who had died in a road accident. Her name was Yaeko Hirai . . . I assume you know her, right?'

Only Nagare replied. 'Yeah.'

Hirai's family ran an old travellers' inn in Sendai, and as the eldest child she had been meant to take over. But she didn't want to, and when she was eighteen, she left to make her own life. Her parents disinherited her. Only her sister stayed in contact. Year after year, she had visited Hirai, trying to persuade her to return home. Then, tragically, she had died in a road accident on the way home from one such visit.

Hirai travelled to the past to meet her sister.

'After visiting her sister in the past, she immediately returned to the inn and took it over. I wanted to hear her side of the story, so I went to Sendai.'

Seven years had passed. Hirai was now thriving as the manager of the inn.

'I asked her, "Why did you go and meet your dead sister, even though you knew that the present would not change?" She laughed at my rude and nosy question, and then said this.

' "If I had led a sad life as a result of my sister's death, then it would have been as if her death had caused it. So, I thought I mustn't allow that to happen. I swore to myself that I would make sure that I was happy. My joy would be the legacy of my sister's life."

'On hearing this, it occurred to me what I had been missing. I had always thought that because my wife had died, I, on my own, should never be happy.'

After he stopped talking, he slowly looked down at the present he was holding in his hands.

'Your wife is no longer with us, then?' Nagare asked in a soft voice.

Kiyoshi seemed determined not to let this news dampen the atmosphere.

'No. But it happened thirty years ago,' he said, trying to tone down the impact.

On hearing this, Kazu asked, 'So it was your late wife's birthday?'

'Yes,' he replied and looked over at the centre table. 'That day, we had arranged to meet here, but I couldn't make it because of work. Back then, none of us had mobile phones, so she waited until closing time. Then, when she was walking home, she got caught up in a mugging that took place in the neighbourhood.'

When he finished talking, he adjusted his hunting cap so that it fitted snugly on his head.

'I'm sorry. I didn't know. I must have sounded rude before . . .' said Nagare, bowing his head low. He now felt bad for questioning Kiyoshi's need to go back to the past just to deliver a gift.

Of course, he wasn't to know that Kiyoshi's wife was dead, so it couldn't be helped. But still, he was chastising himself for acting so rashly.

*I jumped to conclusions when I should have listened to the full explanation.*

'Oh, no, no. On the contrary, I should have explained from the beginning. I'm sorry for the confusion,' Kiyoshi said hurriedly, bowing his head.

'For these thirty years, I have lived with a constant regret. If only I had kept my promise, my wife would not have died, and everything would have been different. But . . .'

He paused, and slowly turned his gaze to Kazu.

'No matter how much I regret it, it won't bring back the dead.'

Moved by Kiyoshi's words, Nagare's eyes widened. He looked at Kazu.

He seemed to want to say something, but he couldn't find his voice. Kazu was staring into the distance in the direction of the woman in the dress. Kiyoshi looked down lovingly at the box that contained the necklace.

'And so, I want to give this to my wife while she was alive,' he said quietly.

*Dong . . . Dong . . . Dong . . .*

The clock on the wall struck eight times, and the sound reverberated through the cafe.

Kiyoshi stood up.

'Please allow me to return to that day when my wife was still alive thirty years ago, her last birthday,' he said, bowing his head deeply.

But Nagare's expression remained dark.

'Er, Kiyoshi, there is something you should know . . .' he began. It was obviously something he found difficult to say, and he was struggling with how to word it. 'Um . . . you see . . . well, it's like this . . .'

Kiyoshi cocked his head to one side, looking at Nagare. It was Kazu who spoke next, with her regular cool expression.

'Well, due to certain circumstances, it is no longer possible to return to the past under my pouring,' she stated.

While Nagare clearly found the situation awkward, Kazu spoke matter-of-factly as if announcing that the lunch menu had finished.

'Oh . . .' Kiyoshi appeared to be stunned by the news. 'Well, if that's the case,' he muttered and slowly closed his eyes.

'Kiyoshi . . .'

He turned to Nagare, who was beginning to say something.

'No, no, that's fine . . . I sort of sensed that there was some issue when I came in just now,' he said with a smile. 'It's disappointing of course, but it can't be helped, right?'

He was doing his best not to let his disappointment show, letting his gaze wander around the room for no reason and avoiding eye contact with the others. It would have been reasonable for him to ask why he couldn't return to the past. But he didn't. Even if he had, his detective's instinct, which he had honed over his long career, told him that he would not get an answer, so there was no point in hanging around. He had no wish to waste their time. He nodded politely.

'. . . Well, I guess you were just about to close,' he said, reaching for his zipped portfolio to put away the birthday present.

Just then . . .

*Flap!*

The sound of the woman in the dress shutting her novel echoed throughout the room.

'Oh,' said Kiyoshi involuntarily.

The woman in the dress rose slowly and started walking towards the toilet without making a sound. The chair was vacant. A person sitting there could travel to the time of their choice. Kiyoshi couldn't help but be completely preoccupied by the empty chair. But then he remembered. *There is no one to pour the coffee.*

He thought it was a shame, but there was no point dwelling on things one couldn't control.

'. . . Well, I guess I'll be off then.' Kiyoshi bowed to Kazu and Nagare, and turned to leave the cafe.

'Kiyoshi, wait,' Nagare called out to him. 'Please give that present to your wife.'

Kiyoshi looked confused for a moment as he pondered Nagare's words.

'But if Kazu cannot pour the coffee, how would that be possible?'

'It's possible . . .'

'I'm sorry, what do you mean?'

Over the last year, Kiyoshi had become well versed in the rules for returning to the past. One of the things he had learned was that only the women of the Tokita family were able to pour the coffee for returning to the past.

'Wait just a minute,' said Nagare as he disappeared into the back room.

When Kiyoshi looked at Kazu in puzzlement, she said calmly, 'I'm not the only woman in the Tokita family . . .'

*How could there possibly be another woman at this cafe that I have never met?*

As Kiyoshi was trying to work out who it could be, he heard Nagare in the back room. 'Come on, hurry up!'

Then he heard a second voice.

'Finally, *moi*'s turn has arrived!'

It was a young girl's voice, speaking in a rather peculiar tone.

'. . . Ooh,' said Kiyoshi as he recognized it.

'Thank you for waiting, monsieur!' Miki said in an unexpectedly loud voice as she entered the cafe. Kiyoshi had assumed that only grown-up women could serve the coffee.

'Is it you, monsieur, who wants to return to the past?'

'Miki, please, speak proper Japanese,' said Nagare, aghast at her attitude. But Miki tsk-tsked him with a wave of her finger.

'That is not possible, *moi* is not Japanese,' she retorted.

Nagare gave an exaggerated frown as if he had been expecting such a response. 'Oh, what a shame! It is a rule of the cafe that the person who pours the coffee must be Japanese.'

'Only kidding! I'm Japanese!' she exclaimed, flip-flopping shamelessly.

With a sigh of exasperation Nagare said, 'Yes, yes. We all know that. Hurry up and get ready.'

He motioned with his hand for her to go to the kitchen.

'OK,' Miki replied enthusiastically and hurried off.

While this exchange was taking place, Kazu appeared

completely detached, standing quietly as if she wasn't even present in the room.

'Kazu, help her please,' Nagare called out.

'Yes, sure,' Kazu said. She excused herself from Kiyoshi with a bow and silently vanished into the kitchen.

After watching her go, Nagare turned to Kiyoshi.

'Er, I'm sorry . . .' he said as a way of apologizing for Miki's messing around when Kiyoshi wanted to return to the past to meet his dead wife. But Kiyoshi hadn't been bothered by it, at all. He had found the exchange between Miki and Nagare amusing, heart-warming even. Besides, he was just happy to learn that he could return to the past. His heart raced in anticipation.

Kiyoshi looked at the vacant chair.

'It never even occurred to me that Miki would pour my coffee,' he said.

'Last week she turned seven,' Nagare replied, looking towards the kitchen.

'Oh, now that you mention it . . .' Kiyoshi said, suddenly recalling.

The pourer of the coffee not only had to be a woman of the Tokita family, she also had to be at least seven years of age. Kazu had once told him this. At the time, he hadn't considered it especially important information and had forgotten it.

Kiyoshi again looked to the chair that would take him back in time and began walking towards it, as if it was pulling him.

*I'm going back to the past.*

The thought made his chest feel hot. He looked at Nagare.

'Go ahead and sit down . . .' Nagare urged.

Kiyoshi drew a deep breath and slowly edged his way between the table and the chair. His heart raced even faster.

He sat down in the chair and pulled out the gift that he had just stowed in his portfolio.

'Kiyoshi,' Nagare called as he walked towards him, one eye still on the kitchen.

'Yes, what is it?' Kiyoshi asked, lifting his head up.

Nagare stooped down low and whispered with his hand up against Kiyoshi's ear as if telling secret information.

'About Miki, it will be her first time pouring the coffee. I think you can expect her to be a bit over the top. She will probably lecture you on all the rules. I'm sorry about that, but do you think you could just go along with it?'

Kiyoshi understood perfectly what Nagare, as a father, was asking. 'Yes, of course.' He smiled.

A moment later, Miki returned from the kitchen and approached them, taking little steps. She was not dressed in the bow tie and sommelier's apron that Kazu wore when she poured the coffee. Instead, she was wearing her favourite cherry-blossom-pink dress with a wine-red apron over it. The apron, which had been her mother Kei's, fitted her well thanks to Nagare's tailoring.

Miki held the tray bearing the silver kettle and white coffee cup unsteadily, her jerky walk making the cup rattle on the saucer.

Kazu stood at the kitchen entrance, watching over her.

When Miki reached Kiyoshi's side, Nagare spoke.

'Miki,' he began, 'from now on, you will take Kazu's place

in serving coffee to the customers who sit in this chair. Are you willing to do this?'

He spoke with a reverent tone.

*Finally, this day had arrived.*

His innocent little girl was going to take on a special role. Judging by his serious expression, he felt like a father giving away the bride at a wedding. Miki, however, was taking no notice of what he might be thinking. She was putting all her concentration in not letting the cup and kettle on the tray fall.

'Uh? What?' she replied impatiently. She neither understood Nagare's sentiment, nor grasped the importance of the task at hand.

Observing that she was struggling with all her might to do the job of pouring the coffee, Nagare realized that she was still a child – a thought that made him happy.

'It's OK. Nothing . . .' he said with a little sigh. 'Keep at it, you're doing fine,' he muttered, his eyes showing a hint of a smile.

Miki, however, had no time for his comments.

'Do you know the rules?' She had turned to Kiyoshi and begun the explanation. Kiyoshi glanced over to Nagare questioningly and Nagare gave a small silent nod. Kiyoshi turned back to Miki.

'Could you explain them to me? I'll take the cup and tray if you like,' he replied kindly.

She nodded deeply and then gave him the tray. Holding only the silver kettle, she began to explain the rules.

As Kiyoshi was already familiar with the rules, Miki's explanation was over in just two or three minutes.

She forgot to explain the rule that you cannot get up off the chair, and there were other places where she didn't explain everything fully, but Nagare let it go. *He knows the rules, so it will be fine*, he thought.

Miki seemed pleased with how she had explained the rules, as she turned to Nagare with a proud smile and expelled a 'humph' of triumph through her nose.

'Splendid,' Nagare said immediately but added, 'but don't keep Kiyoshi waiting!'

'OK!' Miki replied happily and turned back to Kiyoshi. 'Shall we continue?'

Up until now, when Kazu had poured the coffee, these words had carried with them a serious air, so much so that the temperature of the cafe seemed to drop a little.

However, it was different with Miki. Her smiling expression was lovely, like a mother looking lovingly at her baby. Her smile radiated warmth and seemed out of place on a seven-year-old girl. If people had auras whose colours were somehow visible, there is no doubt that Kazu would be surrounded by pale aqua, while Miki's would be orange. This was how warm and welcoming the atmosphere around her was.

When she smiled, it seemed that the temperature had risen slightly.

*Her smile is as radiant as the spring sun's rays*, Kiyoshi thought. 'Yes, let's,' he said, nodding.

'OK,' replied Miki. 'REMEMBER, BEFORE THE COFFEE GETS COLD!'

Shouting boisterously, her voice reverberated around the room.

*Way too loud . . .* thought Nagare as he gave a wry smile.

Miki held the silver kettle above her head and began pouring. The coffee formed a thin line as it streamed into the bright white cup.

It must have been heavy for seven-year-old Miki to hold up the kettle full of coffee like that. She was doing her best to pour with just one hand, but the spout was swaying from side to side and coffee spilled from the cup, leaving a brown puddle on the saucer.

She was taking it seriously, but her mood was not as serious as when Kazu poured. Her earnest attempt to do her best was heart-warming. While Kiyoshi's attention was fixed on Miki's performance, the cup was filled with coffee and a plume of vapour began to rise.

At that moment, Kiyoshi felt his surroundings beginning to warp as they seemed to waver and shimmer. Being sixty, he was worried that the sudden dizziness was a sign that he was unwell.

*Of all the times for something like this to happen,* he thought. But his concerns were fleeting.

He soon realized that his body was turning into vapour. He was startled, but at the same time, he felt relieved that the dizziness had nothing to do with his health.

His body seemed to billow as his surroundings began flowing past him.

'Oh!' he exclaimed – not because he was startled, but rather because he suddenly realized that he had not even decided yet what he was going to say to his wife, whom he had not met for thirty years, when he gave her the gift.

*I'm sure that Kimiko wouldn't have known you can return to the past in this cafe . . .*

While his consciousness was fading, he considered how he might give her the necklace.

Kiyoshi's wife Kimiko was a woman with a strong sense of right and wrong. She and Kiyoshi had known each other since high school, and they shared the ambition of wanting to join the police force.

However, although they both passed the recruitment exam, the number of female recruits taken on was still low back then and Kimiko never became a police officer. Kiyoshi was assigned the role of police-box constable, but his passion for the job did not go unnoticed: he earned a posting in the First Criminal Investigation Division when he was thirty. When this happened, they had been married for two years. Kimiko was genuinely happy to hear that Kiyoshi was to start work as a detective. Kiyoshi, however, began to doubt whether he was cut out for such a role.

He was warm and friendly. His motivation for joining the police was to serve people. And he wanted to please Kimiko, who had dreamed of becoming a police officer. However, once he had become an officer, he found it a struggle. The First Criminal Investigation Division handled homicide and man-slaughter cases. He was continuously confronted with the dark side of humanity, where people took the lives of others, spurred on by selfish desires or self-preservation. He never felt mentally tough enough to withstand this reality on the strength of his own beliefs and sense of purpose alone. He often thought, *If I go on like this, I'll have a mental breakdown.*

Fearing that he was at breaking point, he had decided to admit to Kimiko that he wanted to quit being a detective. Finding it difficult to bring up the subject at home, he had invited her to the cafe on the pretext of it being her birthday, and was planning to tell her then. But on the chosen date, work came up and he thought, *I'll just tell her another day.* Kiyoshi chose the work that he claimed to hate over going to the cafe. As a result, Kimiko got caught up in the incident that took her life.

A tragic incident was really the only way to describe it. When Kiyoshi didn't turn up at the arranged time, Kimiko waited for him until the cafe closed. After leaving, she turned down a narrow street. It was dark, but it was the shortest route to the station. It was on that street that she encountered a mugger robbing an old woman. Coming face-to-face with a crime taking place, her strong sense of right and wrong made it impossible for her to look the other way. Instead, she decided to try to reason quietly with the mugger, but to do so she had to approach him – carefully. If she gave the mugger cause to panic, he might do anything to the old woman. He had a knife, but she felt confident she could persuade him to stand down once she had his attention. But just at that moment, someone from the other side of the street yelled, 'Hey you! What do you think you're doing?'

When the mugger heard this, he pushed the old woman away and started running as fast as he could in Kimiko's direction. While attempting to run past her, panicking or stumbling, he ended up crashing into her as he held the knife in his hand. It was a box-cutter with a thin disposable type of blade that wouldn't have made much damage if it struck her coat. But as he fell, the knife struck Kimiko's bare neck and severed a carotid artery. She died from loss of blood.

*If only I had kept my promise and was there to look after her . . .*

The impact of this incident on Kiyoshi was profound. Simply walking past the cafe, he experienced severe palpitations. It was a traumatic shock that scarred his heart deeply. Psychological trauma is not visible on the outside, and such wounds do not easily heal, especially for someone like Kiyoshi, who was left thinking that it was his fault that the person he loved died. After all, nothing will bring that person back.

He thought that by breaking his promise, he had caused Kimiko's death. Even if his rational brain accepted another version of reality, his heart never would. Finally, he had succumbed to thinking, *With Kimiko's death on my conscience, what right do I have to happiness?*

But after interviewing the people who had returned to the past at the cafe, he decided that it was time to change.

'Wow, it's true! A man just appeared out of nowhere!' said a male voice. It was the first thing Kiyoshi heard after coming to. He had lost consciousness while travelling back through time. Behind the counter, a man wearing an apron that didn't suit him – and looking like a university researcher performing an experiment – was looking at him. When Kiyoshi looked at the man and made a sign of acknowledgement, the man called out, 'Kaname!' and then shuffled away into the back room.

*He doesn't look suited for the cafe, even for a casual staff member. He must be new?*

While Kiyoshi's train of thought went on in this vein, he looked around the room. Although he was in the cafe thirty years in the past, the interior was no different from the present. Everything, down to the smallest detail, was the same. Nevertheless, he felt confident that he had indeed gone back: the man had called out for Kaname, and he had heard from Kinuyo that Kaname was the name of Kazu's mother.

There didn't seem to be any other customers in the cafe. He was about to sink into his own thoughts when a woman appeared from the back room. She was wearing a reddish-brown apron over a white-collared, floral-patterned dress, and she had an obvious bulge in her stomach.

*She must be . . .*

It was Kaname, pregnant with Kazu.

Kaname smiled.

'Hello, welcome,' she said to Kiyoshi with a quick polite nod. Wearing such a carefree expression, she looked like an entirely different person from the ghost called Kaname who sat in the chair.

*The type of person who could easily break the ice and get on well with anyone.*

That was Kiyoshi's impression of Kaname.

Behind her, he could see a man hiding in her shadow, looking as if he had seen a ghost. Kiyoshi looked apologetic.

'Oh, did I startle someone with my sudden appearance?' he asked Kaname.

'Please excuse us. It was the first time my husband has witnessed someone appearing in that chair.'

Although she was saying this in apology, she did not conceal her amusement. Also, judging by the man's red face, he was embarrassed to have reacted in such a way.

'I'm sorry . . .' he said in a small voice.

'Oh, no need to apologize,' Kiyoshi replied.

*They look happy*, he thought.

'Have you come to meet someone?' Kaname asked.

'Yes, I have,' he replied.

Kaname looked around the empty cafe and showed a sympathetic face.

'It's all right. I know what time she arrives . . .' He looked at the middle of the three clocks on the wall as he spoke, to reassure her that he knew what the actual time was and when the person he was waiting for was due.

'Oh, I see. That's good, then . . .'

She smiled, looking relieved.

The man standing in the background was still regarding Kiyoshi as something mysterious. Kiyoshi had a question.

'Hasn't your husband ever seen you pour the coffee?' There was still a little time before Kimiko would come. He couldn't resist asking Kaname, Kazu's mother, some questions.

'My husband only helps out when he has a day off from work. Also, it is currently no longer possible to return to the past under my pouring,' she replied.

*That's the same expression that Kazu used.*

'It is not possible to return to the past when you pour the

coffee? Why is that?' Kiyoshi found himself asking. It was like the detective in him had been switched on. In his mind, he was smiling at his inability to refrain from asking questions whenever he was the slightest bit unclear on anything.

In reply, Kaname placed her hand on her stomach.

'Because of my baby . . .' She smiled happily.

'Really? Why is that?'

'When a pourer becomes pregnant with a girl, the pourer's power is transferred to the baby . . .'

Kiyoshi's eyes opened in surprise.

'Is it right that your daughter will be able to pour coffee to return people to the past when she turns seven?'

'Yes. That's right! You're quite well informed, aren't you?'

Kiyoshi was no longer listening.

*Kazu is pregnant. Yet she didn't seem the least bit happy.*

If Kazu had been happy about her pregnancy, he thought he would have seen at least a smile like the one Kaname gave standing before him.

*Maybe that's because . . .*

A certain thought struck Kiyoshi's heart.

At that moment . . .

### CLANG-DONG

As the doorbell rang, the clock on the wall chimed.

*Dong, dong, dong, dong, dong . . .*

It was the time when Kimiko would arrive.

Immersed in thoughts of Kazu and Kimiko, Kiyoshi's mind was racing.

'It seems the person you are waiting for has arrived.'

While hearing Kaname's relieved tone, he took a deep breath and decided to do what he came to do.

'I can do this . . .'

Upon observing Kiyoshi mutter this, Kaname signalled with a wink to her husband to go to the back room. She was not willing to risk him becoming a distraction for whoever Kiyoshi had come to meet.

No one had yet entered the cafe, but clearly someone was there.

*. . . Will Kimiko recognize me?*

Kiyoshi's heart was beginning to race.

Kimiko did not know that this was a cafe where you could return to the past. There was therefore no chance that she could imagine the possibility of a sixty-year-old Kiyoshi coming to see her. So, she definitely would not recognize him.

But, just to be sure, he adjusted his tattered hunting cap so that it fitted more snugly on his head as he waited.

'Hello, welcome,' Kaname's voice rang out.

Then a moment later Kimiko entered.

Kiyoshi looked up ever so slightly to get a glimpse of her. She was glancing around the cafe. Then, after slowly removing her thin spring coat, she sat down at the middle of the three tables. Several cherry blossom petals fell from her shoulders and fluttered to the floor. When Kiyoshi looked up, he could see her face front on.

Kaname served Kimiko a glass of water.

'Could I have a coffee, please?' she requested.

'Hot coffee?'

'Yes, please.'

'One hot coffee coming right up.'

As Kaname took the order she glanced over at Kiyoshi. As they locked eyes, she smiled and turned to Kimiko.

'We freshly grind the beans when we make coffee, if you don't mind waiting?' she asked with a hint of excitement in her voice.

'Yes, that's fine. I'm waiting for someone, anyway,' Kimiko replied pleasantly.

'Well then, please relax and enjoy your stay here.'

Kaname looked over at Kiyoshi as she said this. She walked back to the kitchen, seemingly enjoying herself. This left just Kiyoshi and Kimiko in the room. The way they were seated meant they could look at each other. Kiyoshi reached for the cup in front of him and pretended to drink as he studied Kimiko's face.

Thirty years ago had been the peak of Japan's financial boom, and a wide selection of fashions had been in the stores. The women of that time could be seen parading around the city wearing colourful and elaborate clothes. Kimiko, however, was not interested in fashion. That day, under her light coat, she wore a plain outfit: a brown jumper over a grey trouser suit. Nevertheless, her straight posture and shoulder-length hair tied up at the back gave her a dignified air.

From under the peak of his hunting cap, he looked again, this time immediately locking eyes with Kimiko. She smiled at him.

'Hello,' she said.

Kimiko was not shy. If the other person was advanced in age, she would always be the first to offer a greeting. Kiyoshi nodded in return. She didn't seem to have noticed that it was Kiyoshi as an old man sitting in front of her.

*It looks like things will go smoothly . . .*

Kiyoshi decided to go ahead.

'Are you Kimiko Manda?' he asked.

'Huh?'

Kimiko was startled that an old man she didn't know had called her name.

'Yes, that's right . . . and, who are you?' she answered. As you would expect from someone cut out to be a police officer, she responded to the unexpected situation with calm.

'Well actually, a man called Kiyoshi Manda gave me this to give to you . . .'

'That's from my husband?'

'Yes.'

Upon saying this, Kiyoshi looked like he was about to stand up from the chair to give her the present.

'Aahh! Aahh! Sir!' someone shrieked loudly in alarm at Kiyoshi. 'Stop right there! You know you shouldn't do that!' said Kaname as she approached him with a hand cradling her stomach. Both Kiyoshi and Kimiko looked at her, startled by the sudden loud voice.

'Sir, didn't you just say you have a slipped disc and can hardly walk?' Kaname said to him with a wink.

'Oh!'

Kiyoshi had completely forgotten about the rule that while in the past you couldn't stand up from the chair. If he had even taken his bottom off the seat, he would have been returned to the future by force.

'Ah! Yeow! Ooh, that hurt . . .' He hurriedly placed his hand on his lower back and feigned a grimace of pain.

The acting may not have fooled everyone, but Kimiko didn't seem to suspect.

'What? You've herniated a disc? Are you all right?'

'Yes . . . I'm fine,' he answered, admiring how Kimiko was so kind to anyone without prejudice. He found himself holding back tears.

Kimiko genuinely cared about everyone, and she showed kindness to anyone. During such times, she never hesitated and always proceeded with complete confidence. Some people thought her actions were those of a nosy do-gooder, but that didn't worry her. She was always the first person to give up her seat on a train for a pregnant woman or an elderly person, and if she saw someone looking lost on a street corner, she would ask if they needed help.

Kimiko didn't do this because she had wanted to be a police officer. It was just in her nature. This side of her personality was what had attracted Kiyoshi most when they were high-school students.

'Are you sure you're all right?' Kimiko asked him with concern.

'Yes, thank you,' he replied unnaturally, averting his eyes.

He was defensive not because he was worried that his lie would be revealed, but rather out of concern that Kimiko's irresistible kindness would penetrate his heart.

'Well, be careful now, won't you,' said Kaname to Kiyoshi. 'Oh, and the coffee is better while it's hot . . .' she added before going into the kitchen again.

Kiyoshi looked at Kimiko apologetically.

'Sorry about that,' he said with a nod.

But rather than sitting down again, she asked, looking at his hands, 'So is that what you were about to give me?'

'Er, yes . . .'

Kiyoshi hastily held out the box for her to take.

Kimiko accepted it and looked at it quizzically. 'What could this be?'

'It's your birthday, isn't it?'

'Huh?'

'Today.'

'Uh-huh.'

Kimiko's eyes widened in surprise and looked hard at the box in her hands.

'. . . Your husband told me he desperately wanted you to enjoy this gift today. He said there was some emergency and he had to travel up north, and before he rushed off, he asked me to give it to you. He was in here just thirty minutes ago.'

This was happening at a time when the average person didn't walk around town with a mobile phone or pager. If it was necessary to cancel a date, then the person would have to call the place of the meeting directly or get an acquaintance to pass on a message. If neither was possible, then the person would simply be left waiting for hours.

Kiyoshi frequently had to change his schedule because of urgent police business, and sometimes, when he had a date with Kimiko, he asked strangers to pass on the message. So, even though she had been told by this old stranger that her husband had asked him to give her this present, she did not appear surprised.

'Oh, really?' she muttered as she noisily tore open the

wrapping paper. Inside was a necklace with a very tiny diamond. Until then, Kiyoshi had never given Kimiko a birthday present. Partly this was because he was always too busy to find the time, but it was also because Kimiko had been mildly traumatized by birthdays in the past.

Her birthday was on the first of April: April Fool's Day. When she was a child, friends would often give her a present, say, *Happy birthday*, then immediately say, *April fool*, and take the present away. They probably didn't mean to be nasty, but Kimiko found being called an April fool straight after the elation of thinking she was about to receive a present very upsetting. Kiyoshi had witnessed her in such a state back in high school.

It was the first of April, the cherry blossoms were in bloom and school was on spring break. Her class friends had met to wish Kimiko happy birthday. Upon giving her a present, they shouted, *April fool!* Of course, her friends didn't do it to be mean, and they immediately handed the present back to her after the joke.

Kimiko said, *Thank you*, with a smile, but for a moment Kiyoshi had glimpsed the sadness that she was attempting to hide. If he hadn't been so fond of her, he probably would not have noticed. Even after they were going steady, Kimiko made other arrangements and avoided being in a position where she might receive a birthday present. Despite that, Kiyoshi wanted to wish her happy birthday properly, on her last one at least, and decided to travel back in time to do it.

Kimiko looked at the necklace.

'Happy birthday . . .' said Kiyoshi softly.

At this remark Kimiko looked at him in surprise.

'Did my husband say that?'

'Huh? Yes . . .'

As soon as she heard his reply, large tears began to flow from her eyes. Kiyoshi began to feel agitated seeing her cry like that. It was the first time since they had met that he had seen her tearful face. He had always seen her as the strong woman who would remain unshakeable in the face of anything. Even after being told on multiple occasions that she had not been accepted into the police force because of the limited number of openings for women officers, she had never cried. She simply said with grit and determination, *I'll get in next time*. That was the Kimiko that Kiyoshi had known. So, seeing her cry like this was beyond his comprehension.

'Wha-what's wrong?' he asked nervously.

He didn't know whether she would open up to a complete stranger. But he desperately wanted to know the reason for her tears.

'Sorry, you'll have to forgive me,' she muttered. Returning to the table where she had been sitting, she took a handkerchief from her bag and began wiping her tears as if trying to stem the flow. Kiyoshi looked at her anxiously. She sniffed, put on a brave face and smiled.

'Well, the truth is that I thought my husband was going to break up with me today,' she said.

'. . . What?' Kiyoshi couldn't believe what he was hearing. Her words were totally unexpected.

It was such a shock, he thought, *Have I travelled back to a completely alternative reality?*

'Oh, umm . . .'

Although he felt the need to say something, no words

came from his mouth. To play for time, he grabbed the coffee cup and took a sip of coffee. Clearly much cooler than just a while ago, it was no more than lukewarm.

'If I am not intruding, could you elaborate a little?' The request that popped out of Kiyoshi's mouth was an expression he often used. It made Kimiko chuckle.

'You sound like a detective!' she observed with tear-reddened eyes.

'Only if you feel comfortable talking to me about it, of course . . .'

He had slipped for a moment into using police lingo, but he felt unable to return to the present without some explanation for Kimiko's tears. Sometimes people will only confide in someone they trust, but other times they need the listener to be a complete stranger.

Kiyoshi did not say anything more. He simply waited for Kimiko to respond. He couldn't exactly insist that she tell him. Time was running out, but he had a feeling she would reply. Kimiko stood in front of the table she had been sitting at.

The silence was broken by Kaname arriving with a delicious-smelling coffee.

'Shall I put it here?' She resourcefully placed the coffee not on the table where Kimiko was sitting but instead on the one where Kiyoshi sat.

Kimiko did not hesitate in her reply. 'That will be fine.'

Kaname placed the coffee and the bill on Kiyoshi's table and once again stepped off into the kitchen.

Gripping her bag, Kimiko walked over to Kiyoshi's table.

'Do you mind if I join you?' she asked with one hand on the chair facing him.

'No, of course not,' Kiyoshi replied with a smile. '. . . So?' he prompted.

She took a quiet, deep breath.

'For the last six months or so, my husband has constantly looked grim, and we haven't had one proper conversation,' she began.

'He is often not home because of work, and lately, even when he is home, all he says is, *uh-huh, OK, sure, sorry, I'm tired tonight* . . .'

She once again brought her handkerchief to her eyes.

'Today, he told me he had something important to discuss. I thought that for sure he was going to say he wanted to end the marriage,' she quavered.

Kimiko looked at the necklace she received from Kiyoshi.

'I was sure that he had forgotten my birthday . . .'

Covering her drooping face with both hands, her shoulders began to heave.

Kiyoshi tried to take in what he was hearing. He had never once thought about splitting up. But presented with Kimiko's account, he could see how she could have interpreted it that way. At the time, he had been swamped with a load of big cases, and his lack of sleep and rest never seemed to end. At the same time, he was doubly burdened by his own doubt that he was cut out to be a detective. He had been avoiding any kind of conversation with her out of fear that he would reveal that he was thinking of quitting. He saw now how she could have interpreted his attitude as symptomatic of feeling unhappy in the marriage.

*I feel terrible that I gave that impression . . .*

We can never truly see into the hearts of others. When people get lost in their own worries, they can be blind to the feelings of those most important to them. Kiyoshi didn't know what he should say to his wife crying in front of him. He was currently pretending to be just a stranger who happened to be in the cafe on this day. Moreover, in just a few hours from now, she would lose her life. Although he knew it would happen, there was nothing he could do.

He reached out slowly and picked up the cup. Judging by the temperature of the cup against his palm, the coffee was nearly cold. The next moment, he found himself saying words that even took him by surprise.

'After I married you, I never once thought of breaking up.'

He knew he could not change reality. However, the thought that Kimiko was going to die with such unease lingering was more than he could bear. He didn't care whether she believed him or not, he wanted to reveal his identity and dismiss just one cause of her suffering. Only he could do this.

'I've come from thirty years in the future . . .' he announced to Kimiko, who was staring at him wide-eyed. 'The important matter I wanted to tell you was about something else.'

He gave a little cough and sat up straight. Feeling embarrassed and apologetic as Kimiko stared at him intensely, he pulled his cap further over his head.

'The truth is, I planned on telling you that I wanted to give up being a detective,' he explained. He had the peak of the cap covering his eyes, so he could not see how Kimiko was reacting to his story. Nevertheless, he continued.

'Every day, I had to visit murder scenes and deal with deplorable human beings . . . I was tired of it. I'd see those depraved killers who think nothing of hurting children and the elderly. It made me feel more than sad; despair is a better word . . . it was tough. No matter how much effort we put into our work, none of it stops the crimes from occurring. I began to wonder, why am I doing this to myself, what good is it? But I thought that if I told you this . . . well, I thought you would be angry. So, I kept putting off the conversation . . .'

There must have been only a short time left before the coffee was completely cold. It didn't matter to him whether Kimiko believed him; he simply wanted to say what he thought he should have said.

'But, don't worry. I never quit being a detective . . .' he said, taking a deep breath.

'And we never separated . . .' he added softly.

Kiyoshi was lying with desperate abandon. He noticed his palms were soaking wet. Kimiko had not yet responded. He just stared at the cup in front of him, unable to do anything else. But he had said what he needed. He was too afraid to look at Kimiko's face in fear of what it might show, but he had no regrets.

'. . . My time is up, I must go now,' he said. But as he reached for his cup, she spoke.

'I knew it . . . Kiyoshi, is that really you?'

He could tell from the tone of her voice that she was still in disbelief. But hearing her say his name reminded him of how she had called him that since they were in high school.

Hearing it brought a warm glow to his eyes. Yet she had

said she'd known, which confused him. He didn't think she knew that this cafe allowed you to return to the past.

'How did you know?'

'Your hunting cap . . .'

'Oh . . .'

The tattered hunting cap he was wearing was a present from Kimiko. She had it custom-made for him when he first became a detective.

She looked at it.

'I see you've worn it a lot,' she said with a smile.

'Yeah.'

More than thirty years had passed since he received it as a present. Now, he couldn't imagine not wearing it.

'Your work must have been tough.'

'Yeah, I guess.'

'Why didn't you quit?' she asked, her voice trailing off.

The real reason was because he couldn't free himself from the guilt of believing that he was to blame for Kimiko getting caught up in the mugging, by not turning up to meet her. Going on being a detective was his way of punishing himself for ever. In reply to the question, Kiyoshi looked straight into her eyes.

'You were there for me . . .' he replied.

'I was?'

'Uh-huh.'

'Really?'

'Uh-huh,' he replied without hint of doubt or hesitation. Sensing something in the corner of his vision, he turned to see Kaname looking at him. She simply blinked once, subtly.

*You'd better go very soon.*

Kiyoshi understood exactly what that blink meant. He looked at Kaname with a hand on her large stomach and remembered Kazu.

*Kazu and I, our situations are similar.*

Kiyoshi gave a small nod to Kaname and looked down at the cup.

'Well, I have to return now.'

'Kiyoshi . . .'

Kimiko called his name as he brought the cup to his mouth. She had realized from the exchange between him and Kaname that it was time to say goodbye.

'. . . and were you happy?' she asked, her voice trailing off.

'Of course,' he replied and drank the entire cup in one gulp. As he tasted it, his heart skipped a beat. The coffee was already cooler than body temperature.

*If Kaname had not distracted me right now, the coffee might have gone cold.*

Kiyoshi looked over at Kaname, and she returned an indescribably wonderful smile.

He was engulfed in dizziness. His surroundings slowly started moving past him. A moment later his body was turning into white vapour.

'Thanks . . .'

He saw Kimiko clutching the necklace to her chest.

'. . . for this.'

She was looking at Kiyoshi, smiling happily.

'It suits you!' he remarked in his bashful shy way. But he never knew whether his words reached her.

'He's back!' Miki exclaimed loudly as Kiyoshi regained consciousness.

Miki looked around and smiled broadly at Nagare. The first customer she had sent back to the past had returned. She looked immensely pleased with herself. Nagare too let out a sigh of relief. He gently fondled Miki's head. 'Good job.'

Only Kazu maintained her always cool expression as she started to clear away Kiyoshi's cup for Miki, who was still very excited.

'How was it?' she asked.

'So, you're pregnant?' he replied.

*Crash, clang-clang-clang . . .*

The noisy sound of a tray dropping onto the floor rang through the cafe. The culprit was Nagare.

'Daddy! Don't be so noisy!' Miki scolded him.

'So sorry . . .' he said, quickly picking up the tray.

Kazu's expression hardly changed.

'Yes, I am,' she answered.

'. . . How did you know that?' asked Nagare.

'I met your mother while she was pregnant with you,' Kiyoshi explained, looking at Kazu. 'Your mother told me that she couldn't act as coffee pourer while she was pregnant.'

'Oh, did she?' Kazu said as she walked off to the kitchen to take away the cup that Kiyoshi had used.

At that moment, the woman in the dress, Kaname, appeared from the toilet. Kiyoshi stood up and gave her a short bow. As he gave up the seat, Kazu returned from the kitchen carrying a coffee for Kaname.

As she placed the coffee down in front of her, Kiyoshi said to her softly, 'Your mother looked happy.'

Kazu stopped moving after she'd placed the cup on the table.

It was for no more than a second. Both Nagare and Kiyoshi waited anxiously for Kazu's response before Miki saved everyone from an awkward silence.

'Ah!' said Miki. 'Look!'

She crouched down and picked something up from the floor. Clenched between her thumb and index finger was a single cherry blossom petal. It must have been carried in on someone's head or shoulder.

Glimpsing a single flower petal is another way of noticing spring.

Miki held out the petal in her fingers.

'Spring is here!' she announced, and Kazu smiled gently.

'Ever since that day when Mum never returned from the past . . .' Kazu began, in a calm voice. 'I was always afraid of being happy.'

She spoke as if she was telling this to someone other than those around her. In fact, it seemed as though she was addressing the cafe itself.

'That was because on that day, when my mother suddenly disappeared . . . the constant stream of happy days and the happiness of the person most precious to me just came to an end.'

Tears began to stream down her face.

Since the day Kaname had failed to return from the past, Kazu had never made any friends, not even at school. The fear of losing them was too great. She never joined a club or formed part of a clique, not in junior high or high school. Even if she was invited to play, she never went. After school finished, she immediately returned to the cafe, where she would help out. She had no relationship with anyone and showed no interest in others. Behind this all was her thought: *I cannot be happy.* All her life, this was what she had been telling herself.

She devoted herself to the cafe. She did not ask for anything else, she did not hope for anything else. She only lived to pour coffee. That was her way of punishing herself for what happened to her mother.

Tears sprang from Nagare's eyes. They were the tears of a man who had been by Kazu's side constantly since that day, watching over her.

'I was the same,' Kiyoshi said. 'If I had not broken our date, my wife might not have died. I thought that her death was my fault for not meeting her. I didn't think I deserved to be happy.'

Kiyoshi had likewise become a slave to his work as a detective. He deliberately chose a hard path for himself. He was imprisoned by the thought: *I don't deserve happiness.*

'But I was wrong. I learned this from the people I met through this cafe.'

He hadn't only interviewed Kaname, and Hirai, who had gone back to see her dead sister. He had also talked to a woman who had gone back to see the boyfriend she had broken up with, and a woman who had gone back to see her husband whose memory was fading. Then there was the man who went back the previous spring to see his close friend who died twenty-two years before, and the man who went back the previous autumn to see his mother who died in hospital. Then in the winter, a man who knew he was dying came from the past to bring happiness to the lover he left behind.

'I found the words that he left behind particularly touching.'

Kiyoshi brought out his small black notebook and read aloud.

' "If you try to find happiness after this, then this child will have put those seventy days towards making you happy. In that case, its life has meaning. You are the one who is able to create meaning for why that child was granted life. Therefore, you absolutely must try to be happy. The one person who would want that for you the most is that child."

'In other words, the way I live my life creates happiness for my wife.'

Kiyoshi had read those words over and over so many times, just that one page in his notebook was creased and stained.

These words also seemed to strike a chord with Kazu – a new stream of tears began to flow.

Kiyoshi put the notebook away in his jacket pocket and pulled down his hunting cap to fit more snugly on his head.

'I do not think it is at all possible that your mother didn't return so that you would be miserable. So, have your baby . . . and . . .'

He took a deep breath and turned to Kazu, who was looking at Kaname.

'You're allowed to be happy,' he added.

Without saying anything, Kazu slowly closed her eyes.

'Well, thanks for the coffee.' Kiyoshi placed the money on the counter and walked towards the exit. Nagare gave a small nod in reply.

'Oh . . .' Kiyoshi said, suddenly turning round.

'Forget something?' asked Nagare.

'No . . .' he replied and turned to Kazu.

'That necklace you helped choose, my wife really loved it,' he said, and with a bow of the head, he went out.

### CLANG-DONG

Once again, silence filled the cafe.

Miki, no doubt relieved that her work was done, started nodding off while holding Nagare's hand.

'Oh, of course.'

Nagare realized why Miki had suddenly grown so quiet. He picked her up with an 'alley-oop'.

The cherry blossom petal, released from Miki's fingers, fluttered to the ground.

'Spring, huh?' he muttered.

'Big brother . . .'

'Hmm?'

'I . . . I guess I'm allowed to be happy, aren't I?'

'Yeah, of course. She can take over from you now . . .'

Nagare readjusted Miki in his arms.

'No problem at all . . .' he said, walking off into the back room.

'. . . Hmm.'

A long winter was about to end.

The interior had remained unchanged since that day.

'Mum . . .'

Hanging from the ceiling, the wooden fan rotated slowly.

'I'm . . .'

The three large clocks on the wall each showed different times. The shaded lamps tinted the interior with a sepia hue.

Kazu drew in a deep breath in this cafe where time seemed to stand still and placed her hand on her stomach.

'I am going to be happy,' she exclaimed.

As she said this, Kaname, while still looking down at her novel, smiled warmly. It was the same smile that Kaname had given Kazu when she was alive.

'Mum?' said Kazu, and at that moment Kaname's body, like vapour rising from freshly poured coffee, rose upwards.

The vapour hung in the air for a moment and then simply vanished into the ceiling.

Kazu slowly closed her eyes.

Kaname had disappeared and a gentleman in his early old age was sitting in the chair. He picked up the novel that was left on the table and turned to the first page.

'I'll have a coffee, if I may?' he said to Kazu.

For a moment, she stood motionless, silently staring up at the ceiling. Then she finally slowly looked down at the gentleman.

'. . . Certainly, I'll go and make it,' she said and walked off sprightly to the kitchen.

Seasons flow in a cycle.

Life too, passes through difficult winters.

But after any winter, spring will follow.

Here, one spring had arrived.

Kazu's spring had just begun.